THE
WIKKELING

Steven Arntson

Illustrated by
Daniela Jaglenka Terrazzini

RP KIDS
PHILADELPHIA • LONDON

For my parents,

HELEN & JERRY

Books published by Running Press are available at special discounts for bulk purchases
in the United States by corporations, institutions, and other organizations.
For more information, please contact the Special Markets Department at
the Perseus Books Group, 2300 Chestnut Street, Suite 200, Philadelphia, PA 19103,
or call (800) 810-4145, ext. 5000, or e-mail special.markets@perseusbooks.com.

ISBN 978-0-7624-3903-4

Library of Congress Control Number: 2010935091

E-book ISBN 978-0-7624-4249-2

9   8   7   6   5   4   3   2   1

Digit on right indicates the numbers of this printing

Cover and interior design by Frances J. Soo Ping Chow

Edited by T. L. Bonaddio

Typography: Blackadder, Blavicke Capitals, Praeton, Requiem, Riva

Published by Running Press Kids

an imprint of Running Press Book Publishers

A Member of the Perseus Books Group

2300 Chestnut Street

Philadelphia, PA 19103-4371

Visit us on the web!

www.runningpress.com

Acknowledgements

When a book first sprouts, it feels quite independent, but it is quickly humbled by its needs and indebted for its very existence to those who helped it. Firstly, a thank-you to the members of my writing group for looking at my earliest efforts. My agent, Jenni Ferrari-Adler, went far above and beyond the call of duty in helping me revise and in taking up the cause of the book. My editors Teresa Bonaddio, Marlo Scrimizzi, and Kelli Chipponeri were of tremendous aid in believing in the project and bringing the characters to life through numerous patient rounds of revision. I'd also like to thank Daniela for the beautiful illustrations and Frances Soo Ping Chow for the wonderful cover and book design—they've placed me in the enviable position of having my name attached to something much more beautiful than I'd ever imagined. More than anyone, however, I'm indebted to my wife Anne Mathews, who has, during the course of our marriage and friendship, been the greatest influence on how I think and what I think about. Without our countless conversations about life and the living of it, and without her example, this book would not have been conceived. She also gave the manuscript its first real copyedit, caused the sentences to become readable, and pointed out several directions in which I had forgotten to look (as all who know me know, and she best of all, my eyes are very poor). Thank you, for reading.

Poor kitty,
poor kitty!
The Wikkeling chased you
From city to country
And back again, too.
It won't rest. It won't weary.
It will kill you, poor kitty,
And then all those like you,
And all those you knew.

Jump up to my attic
Poor kitty, and pause—
Rest here. Recover,
And sharpen your claws.
I'll give you refuge
For I understand
What it is to be hunted,
Unwelcome, unwanted,
Pursued and tormented
And fainting from fear
Every night,
Every night,
Every night of the year.

—Anonymous, from Aristotle Alcott's
Riddles and Rhymes of Olden Times

Prologue

The Old City lies on a long, low hill. It is dangerous and dilapidated. The buildings are crumbling, moss grows in the streets, and garbage festers in the gutters. There are rumors that people live here secretly, breaking into abandoned apartments and living wretched, illegal lives.

Adjoining the Old City is the Addition, which lies on a vast, level plain. The Addition sparkles into the haze, its streets as straight as grocery store aisles, its buildings as shiny as pop cans. The Addition contains countless homes, businesses, schools, and hospitals. Skyscrapers rise in lanky rectangles. Sprawling suburban chessboards meet the broad blocks of industry. The Addition is so large that airports operate to fly people from one part to another.

Between the Old City and the Addition runs a seam, where the decrepit hill meets the youthful plain. Few people know it, but this seam is the kind of place where unexpected things happen. Invisible doors and windows open. Unknown creatures appear. Even now, something strange is afoot.

●·····●

It's past midnight, but this street, called Boardwalk, is crammed with bumper to bumper traffic. Lilac-scented exhaust fills the air and curls under streetlights and headlights as employees commute to night-shift jobs or return from day-shift jobs, parents take sick children to hospitals, and everyone weaves from lane to lane hoping to dodge the next snarl. Delivery vans deliver new shoes, cell phones, and ready-to-eat dinners to one side of the street while garbage trucks collect old shoes, broken cell phones, and leftovers from the other side. Eighteen wheelers stacked with shipping containers, petroleum tanks, prefab houses, cars, and even new eighteen wheelers pass through on their long-distance routes. In a city as large as this one, there is no time of day or night when such things aren't happening.

Although the Addition seems alive with activity at first glance, it is strangely motionless. Work to home and home to work. Old shoes to new shoes. Delivery and pickup. Repetition becomes stillness, lulling everyone, and this is why no one notices when, in the middle of the street, a shadow the size of a small animal darts from beneath a garbage truck and under a car in the next lane. It dashes across another lane, and then another, camouflaged by a black belch from a tailpipe.

This stretch of Boardwalk is lined with identical, brand-new multi-level houses, constructed of vinyl and glue, sitting behind green plastic lawns. The houses have flat roofs and few windows. They are airtight and soundproof. Someone looking to sneak in would have a tough time. The shadow darts past, slowing at each home and then moving on.

But there is one exception on this block. There's one home made of wood and nails instead of plastic and glue. It's only a single level, and its steeply angled roof rises to a shingled peak, an indication that it was built long ago. Now it's the only one of its kind left here.

The shadow creeps around back, out of the direct glare of the streetlights to a small strip of artificial turf that separates one piece of property from another. It limps, as if injured, but manages a swift, terrific leap to the roof of the old house. It disappears inside through a hole under the eaves.

This old house has a family sleeping within, lying under warm covers, and they are not awakened, soothed as they are by the comforting grind of the endless traffic jam, as monotonous as sheep gliding at intervals over an easy fence. They have no idea that they have a houseguest.

PART 1

Efficient Education

"**S**ENSIBLE STUDENTS SUCCEED SPLENDIDLY!" said Ms. Span, a primly dressed teacher sitting behind a computer at the front of the class, her thick, black eyebrows arching over the top of her reading glasses.

"Yes, Ms. Span!" said the students. They sat in neat rows that filled the room, faces lit yellow from the light of their own computers.

On the wall behind Ms. Span, a large projection displayed the sentence she had just recited. "Let's begin today's focus on the letter S," she said, her voice just loud enough to be heard above the whirring of the fans in all of the computers. The students began to type. Next to each child's screen, a plastic cradle held a cell phone hooked to the school's network. The children's practice sentences were instantly graded and transmitted to their parents' phones, ensuring that each parent knew, at each moment, how their child was scoring.

Additionally, all sentences were tabulated, in terms of accuracy and speed, into a data pool describing the class, the school, the district, and the system as a whole. At this moment, every child everywhere was typing "SENSIBLE STUDENTS SUCCEED SPLENDIDLY," allowing every school to be instantly ranked in comparison to every other school. On Competency Exam days these rankings were used to determine whether or not the school was functioning properly, or whether it should be shut down. Today, fortunately, was not the Competency Exam. It was a Practice Test.

Ms. Span flipped through the students' responses on her screen, checking them. She was on edge, even though it was just practice. The thing about Practice Tests was that they led inevitably to the Competency Exam, and if things went poorly then, Ms. Span could be classified a Bad Teacher and lose her job.

"Very good, Andreas," she muttered. "Very good, Sasha."

Ms. Span projected the next sentence.

"SENSIBLE STUDENTS ARE SAFE, SECURE, AND SUPERVISED!" recited the students, some beginning to type as they spoke. Because the exercises were timed, there was little opportunity to fix mistakes. Ms. Span reviewed the responses again. Her computer screen reflected on her glasses, rankings appearing there in columns.

She glanced at the bottom of the stats and winced at the names there, especially at the one at the very bottom. She frowned. She didn't want to stop the lesson, but the whole class was getting dragged down.

"Miss *Gad-Fly*," she called out frostily. All the children turned toward the rear of the room to look at the object of their teacher's attention. Some of them snickered. Miss Gad-Fly sat in the back row near the door. She seemed lost in thought, and didn't notice the attentions of the room until Ms. Span said, "Henrietta!"

Being singled out scornfully in class wasn't unusual for Henrietta. Wherever she was and whatever she was doing on any given day, she found herself in a similarly unenviable position. If a poll were to be taken this afternoon by her school, asking all the students in all the grades who was least popular, Henrietta Gad-Fly would win. And that would be the only thing she won all year.

Henrietta looked a little like a brick—her face and body were squat, thick rectangles. Her ruddy skin was prone to pimples, and flushed red when she was embarrassed, like now. Her small, black, beady eyes were set closely together, which lent her a confused and peevish expression that often caused people to explain things to her twice, and then scold her. Her thin eyebrows made her look a little surprised, which didn't help matters.

And yet Henrietta was not a stupid, confused, petulant block. Or at least, she didn't feel like one. Inside, she was just herself—a person to whom she'd scarcely yet been introduced.

●·· ··●

Henrietta is the main character of this story. This whole book will be about her—and it's worth mentioning at the outset a few things that aren't going to happen to her.

She will not become beautiful when someone gives her a new hairstyle.

She will not find a miracle cure for her pimples when an angel sees she's a good girl inside.

She will not find out that she's actually a princess, and she won't become happy forever when a prince marries her.

Those books are out there, and your school librarian can help you find one. This isn't it.

•• ••●

"Henrietta," said Ms. Span, "you are *off task*."

With the click of a button, Ms. Span displayed the contents of Henrietta's monitor on the wall screen. Each day contained a moment such as this, in which Henrietta was exposed as an example of the kind of person one should have the common sense not to be. Henrietta, everyone knew, ranked at the bottom of the class in most subjects: writing, reading, math, and even physical safety. Her scores were so low that she was nearly (but not quite) At Risk.

Henrietta's sentence read: SE

What kind of child could so grievously fail in her attempt to type "SENSIBLE STUDENTS ARE SAFE, SECURE, AND SUPERVISED?" The class had a good laugh, but they didn't laugh as hard as they might have. As with any joke, Henrietta's incompetence had grown less funny over time.

"Henrietta, you will stay after class today and retype your practices," said Ms. Span.

"Yes, Ms. Span," said Henrietta, her voice inaudible over the tinny hum of the fans in the computers.

"What?" said Ms. Span.

"YES, MS. SPAN!" said Henrietta. She pressed her lips together in a way that made her look angry, but she was actually feeling humiliated.

"Now, then, everyone," said Ms. Span, "we've fallen behind because of Henrietta. Today is just Practice, but next month is the Competency Exam. If Henrietta delays us then, we'll have to work even faster, with even more accuracy.

Remember, we're graded as individuals *and* as a class. We compete against each other to help each other. Right now, we're in Good Standing. None of you are At Risk, and none are Finished."

A chill ran down the spine of every student when Ms. Span said "Finished." No one wanted that. If the school declared you Finished, that was it. You were kicked out. Your parents would be really, really mad, and you'd become a garbage collector for the rest of your life.

Typing Practice gave way to Composition, and then Math for the remainder of the morning until it was time for History and Nutrition. Ms. Span removed her reading glasses and bade the class stand, and they lined up and followed her into the hallway, quickly completing the short walk past the mural that read: Sensible, Efficient, Education (S.E.E!).

The History and Nutrition Center was a large room filled with four rows of ten divided study carrels. Each seat in each row was cordoned with yellowish brown walls rising from the desktop. Through the rows ran a conveyor belt used to deliver the day's Approved Nutrition while the students watched various historical videos on the carrel dividers.

Henrietta's class entered just as the kindergartners, whose nutrition came a little earlier, were packing up to return to their room. Henrietta waited at the nearest carrel as its occupant prepared to leave: a little girl, who seemed small even for a kindergartner. Henrietta noticed that she was wearing odd clothes. Instead of a polyester outfit with a yellow safety stripe down the back, she wore a brown shirt made of . . . wool? Henrietta had seen wool in a few old TV shows, where people rode on horses or lived on icebergs. It was said to cause rashes.

The girl's dark-skinned arms looked painfully thin as she stuffed some papers into her backpack, zipped it up, and pulled it with some effort over her shoulders. She ran to join her class, her curly black hair bouncing as she exited.

Henrietta settled into the carrel, noting that the one immediately to her left was occupied by the chubby, bespectacled, Clarence Frederick, and the one to her right by the chubby, bespectacled, Clarice Sodje. Both had bullied Henrietta in the past, and she wasn't thrilled to be between them now.

History and Nutrition period was the day's only non-graded learning experience. History, because it wasn't related to anything, wasn't tested during the Competency Exam. Ms. Span said history had a "Noninstrumental Positive Impact," which meant it was good for you but didn't really matter.

It was also good to watch movies while eating, because watching discouraged talking, and talking with one's mouth full was both dangerous and impolite. The History and Nutrition Center was generally very quiet but for the tinny sounds of the movies playing over the speakers in the carrel dividers.

Henrietta had landed in the HENRIFT ANDI carrel. She'd been in this one a few times before, and had seen the movie already, which was called *Founder, Humanitarian, Forward Thinker*. As she sat, the movie began. Henrift Andi, a tall, clean-shaven man with a stovepipe hat, was giving a speech to a crowd of fascinated onlookers.

"We must be courageous enough to look forward without fear, and sensible enough to fear looking backward!" he said, and the crowd cheered through the little speakers. The title came on:

HENRIFT ANDI:
FOUNDER, HUMANITARIAN, FORWARD THINKER

The end of the title was obscured by a little piece of paper. It was a yellow sticky note attached to the screen. Henrietta leaned forward. The square contained a short message scrawled in a beginner's handwriting.

henrift and andi

Henrietta pulled it off of the screen as the movie segued to show Henrift Andi as a little boy, still wearing a stovepipe hat, planting an apple orchard. Henrietta crumpled the note and dropped it in the trash next to the carrel. She thought the kindergartener who had just departed was most certainly the culprit, and she didn't want the tiny girl to get in trouble for vandalism.

Nutrition arrived on the conveyor belt: a cube of corn bread smothered in starchy gravy, some small yellowish carrots with margarine dip, a pile of corn chips, and a glass of apple soda.

"Soon after," said the narrator's calm but engaging voice, "Henrift Andi developed a new breed of apple, which he called Scrumptious!"

Henrietta dipped a corn chip in the margarine. As she brought it to her mouth, a little paper airplane flew over the carrel wall to land squarely atop her corn bread and gravy. On one wing was written:

DUMBIETTA

It had been thrown by Clarence or Clarice. Such airplanes were a common part of Henrietta's History and Nutrition periods. Since most of the kids had watched all of the history movies already, and because they weren't getting graded, they made mischief of one kind or another. Henrietta plucked the craft from her lunch and was about to toss it into the garbage when she stopped suddenly. She felt a strange sensation, like someone was standing next to her. It was a creepy feeling, and it made her heart skip a beat: it was the feeling that preceded one of her headaches.

A moment later, the headache began. It wasn't too bad yet. It was still small. But it might get worse. Henrietta understood, though her parents had never said it aloud, that a headache could get bad enough to kill her. She was one of those kids who might not make it. She might not grow up.

Henrietta fished her pills from her pocket and ate three of them. She waited in perfect stillness, one hand still holding the forgotten airplane. After an unknown amount of time, she noticed that the credits for FOUNDER, HUMANITARIAN, FORWARD THINKER were rolling past on the screen. She turned and saw her classmates lining up behind Ms. Span. Carefully, she stood and joined them.

Henrietta had suffered headaches for a few years, since she and her parents had moved into the old house they lived in now—in fact, her mother thought it was the house's fault, and the doctor they'd seen had agreed, saying kids raised in old homes sometimes became House Sick. The cause was unknown, but something about those old places was not good for children. Maybe some kind of toxin. They were told they should move, but unfortunately they didn't have enough money to live anywhere else at present.

Henrietta's headaches, though supposedly caused by her house, seemed to strike her everywhere but at home, and they always followed the same progression. First, it seemed for an instant like someone was standing next to her. Then the headache began behind her eyes, and either dissipated or grew. Henrietta either felt better or went to the hospital.

Today, she felt better. Though she was hungry because she'd eaten nothing during History and Nutrition, relief swept through her when she returned to the classroom. Such moments of recovery constituted the greatest joys of her life. She was so happy that when Ms. Span resumed the typing practices, she produced exactly what she was supposed to, and didn't become distracted.

●·· ··●

At the end of the school day, Ms. Span displayed the class's statistics: They were in the top forty percent for the district, which meant they were in Good Standing. If they could keep that up, they'd do fine on the Competency Exam, so Ms. Span ended in a good mood.

Henrietta still had to stay after, though. As the other students left to wait for the buses, Henrietta began to retype her practice sentences.

At the front, Ms. Span previewed the following day's System Approved Lessons (SALs) and leafed through Student Statistical Profiles (SSPs) to see if there was any way to leverage a Competitive Advantage Boost (CAB). She was just starting at the school this year, so none of the students knew her very well. She was generally strict, but Henrietta knew another side of her, which sometimes emerged when the two of them were alone during detention after class.

"Henrietta, your work is looking excellent," Ms. Span said, removing her reading glasses and squinting out across the rows of empty desks. "If only you could perform this well *during class*, you'd be one of the top students."

"Thank you, Ms. Span," said Henrietta. She did have a knack for school-work, and the extra practice she endured in detention had further developed the aptitude.

Ms. Span projected Henrietta's detention and classtime statistics next to one another on the screen. "Why do you have such trouble, Henrietta?" she asked. "It isn't sensible."

"I don't know," said Henrietta. Her detention statistics showed her to be extremely fast and accurate, while her class scores were terrible. Even she was a little confused about it. "I just feel . . . nervous, sometimes."

"Because you get made fun of?" said Ms. Span.

"Yes," said Henrietta. But there was more to it than that. After class, when she and Ms. Span were alone, the work seemed more important, and she felt like she and Ms. Span were a team. This never occurred during class, when everyone competed on a curve. To do better during class meant someone else did worse, and to be singled out meant either you were failing or you were causing others to fail. The best success was to remain unnoticed, right in the middle, and that was pretty boring. Henrietta didn't say any of this to Ms. Span, though. Neither of them could change the way the school worked, and earning detention every day, for Henrietta, was a kind of clever solution to the problem. Not that she felt clever. She felt stupid.

When she completed her extra work, she glanced at her cell phone to check the time. She hadn't missed her bus yet.

"Thank you, Ms. Span," she said, standing.

"Thank you for your good effort, Henrietta. Let's try to do better tomorrow, all right?"

"I'll try, Ms. Span," said Henrietta, and she pulled her backpack onto her shoulders and departed for the bus. Ms. Span clicked a button, and her computer screen read:

STUDENT 3421836 LOG OUT CLASSROOM 7434 16.46.345 [UTC]

Henrietta arrived at the parking lot turnaround just as her bus was preparing to leave. One thing she liked about detention was that she didn't have to stand around with the other kids and wait, friendless. She boarded, found a seat, and began to buckle herself in with a lap belt, two shoulder belts, and a head belt, all designed to assure her survival in the worst imaginable crash.

Her cell phone buzzed in her pocket—her mother calling to see if she needed a ride. Fortunately, as soon as she fastened her last buckle, an automated message appeared on her parents' phones:

STUDENT 3421836 SECURED BUS#1056 ETA 16.46.345 [UTC] STOP 342

The blue warning light over her seat extinguished, indicating to the bus driver that she was fully secure. Around her, other kids talked excitedly and amused themselves, making a racket despite their restraints. The master safety light at the front came on, glowing yellow as the front doors closed and the engine rumbled to life. The bus rolled into the traffic jam.

Gridlock wound unceasingly through nearly every part of the Addition. The cars were packed in the streets, coughing out the city's familiar charred, floral scent of exhaust. Its citizenry succeeded splendidly, labored diligently, recreated briefly, saved sensibly, and spent frugally their short lives in the dense grid of interlocked developments.

The bus crept over perfect asphalt surrounded by a fleet of garbage trucks emitting hazy, yellow-brown streams of lilac-scented particulates. Henrietta looked across the aisle to the seat opposite and saw a boy there she didn't recognize. He was her age, with straight black hair and thick, black eyebrows, locked tightly to his seat by the same network of straps that contained Henrietta and everyone else.

As soon as Henrietta's eyes landed on him, he turned to her, as if on cue. "I hate this!" he exclaimed, and without a pause, he unbuckled all of his safety straps. "Yeah!" he shouted, stretching his arms and sticking his legs out into the aisle.

"Put those back on!" said Henrietta.

There were immediate consequences for him. The yellow safety light went out at the front of the bus, and the blue warning light glared to life above his seat. The bus's engine stopped and then the bus stopped. A thousand messages erupted from outside:

"YOUR PARENTS CAN AFFORD A BIGGER, BETTER HOUSE
FOR YOU AT NEWVIEW ESTATES!"

"YOU'RE NEVER TOO YOUNG FOR YOUR FIRST CAR—NOW AT LURMY'S!"

"IS YOUR CELL PHONE A TINCAN? IT BETTER BE!"

These were Honk Ads, activated by all of the drivers whose vehicles were now stuck behind the bus. Each car horn blared a different advertisement, many of them responding to the presence of the school bus by advertising to the children inside.

"EDIBLE CLEANTASTE CORN SOAP—IT'S
THE CANDY OF SOAP!"

Henrietta heard squealing tires as commuters tried to merge into other lanes, and the horns overlapped into nonsense.

The boy froze. He hadn't realized that this would happen, apparently.

"Don't worry," Henrietta whispered to him through the din. "You'll just get a warning. He doesn't want to be off schedule."

The boy shot Henrietta a worried glance as the driver, a large man wearing a yellow jumpsuit, walked back along the aisle, glaring at every pair of children along the way. When he reached the new boy he frowned down at him and said, "Name."

"I forget!" said the boy, grinning ridiculously.

The driver produced a scanner from his belt, pointed it at the boy, and looked at the screen. "Gary," he said.

"Scary!" quipped a child further back on the bus.

"Scary Gary!" said someone else.

"*Scaredy* Gary!" said a third student.

Hilarity ensued. Henrietta laughed too, even though she felt bad for the boy. She knew what it was like to be made fun of, but it also felt kind of good to make fun of someone else for a change.

"Okay, Mister," said the driver. "I'm issuing you a warning for releasing your safety belt, and a detention for insubordination." As he said this, he scribbled with a plastic stylus on the small screen of the scanner. Then he reached out, roughly rebuckled Gary's straps, and lumbered back to the front, restarting the bus and entering traffic again. "**IT'S TIME FOR A LURMY'S EGG SANDWICH!**" one last Honk Ad announced.

"You shouldn't have aggravated him," said Henrietta.

"Thanks for telling me *now*," Gary replied.

"Well, I didn't know you were *stupid*," Henrietta shot back. That was the end of their conversation.

Henrietta soon recognized the familiar streets of her neighborhood. Because her school was nestled into the Addition's perfect grid of streets, the landmarks Henrietta watched for were older buildings, which signaled the closeness of the Old City. Instead of walls of shiny mirrored windows, the older buildings were dull concrete, stained with traffic exhaust. Henrietta's parents often mentioned how ugly such buildings were, but Henrietta liked them because they meant she was almost home.

Usually she was the only one to disembark at her stop, but today as the bus rolled up, she heard another set of straps release as she released hers. When the door opened and she stepped into the aisle, Gary stood as well.

Henrietta tried not to look at him. She exited the bus and walked to the intersection as the driver stopped Gary and lectured him about the importance of safety. She crossed when the signal turned. Then she heard Gary's voice rise over the din behind.

"I'm sorry!" he yelled. Was he talking to the bus driver or her? She didn't wait to find out.

●·····●

Henrietta's house stuck out like a sore thumb on her block. It was the only old house, the only house without a front yard, and the only house with a steep, shingled roof. It had originally belonged to Henrietta's grandmother, who had given it to Henrietta's parents two years ago when she'd married her longtime friend Al and moved with him to Sunset Estates retirement community, far into the Addition. The old house was rundown, leaky, cramped, and full of the strong smell of lilac air freshener, which Henrietta's mother used to cover the dusty, mildewy smells of age.

As Henrietta reached the front door, she saw a moving van parked across the street. Several people were carrying boxes from it into a new house that had been erected the previous week. Henrietta saw Gary turn into the drive and enter the house through the garage. He was her across-the-street neighbor. This meant she might see him the following morning at the bus stop, a prospect she didn't choose to dwell on at the moment.

She crossed the narrow petunia border between the sidewalk and her front door, which opened as she approached to reveal her mother, a woman of medium height with Henrietta's closely spaced eyes, ruddy skin, and blockish body. She wore a pair of tan, fitted pants and a loose, white blouse, which made her somewhat resemble a vanilla ice cream cone. She ushered Henrietta inside and closed the door, shutting out the traffic noise.

"How was school?" she asked, giving Henrietta a brief hug.

"It was okay," said Henrietta.

"No makeup work?"

"I did it fast," said Henrietta as they entered the living room.

"That's good," said her mother. "That's an improvement."

"Hello, Henrietta," said her father from the living room couch, where he watched the large, flat-screen television that hung in a picture frame on the wall. He was a bland, unobtrusive man dressed in jeans and a gray sweater.

The sound was muted on the TV, and the screen showed an advertisement for bathtub cleaner. Henrietta and her mother sat on the couch with her father, Henrietta between the two of them.

An animated soap bubble gleefully ate the scum ring from around the inside of a bathtub, and then the news resumed. Her father reactivated the sound to listen to the lead story, in which a family who lived in an old house was crushed when it fell in on them. The next story featured a boy who was scratched across the eyes by a cat. The scratch got infected, and the boy had to have his eyeballs amputated.

The ads returned, and Henrietta's dad muted them.

"Henrietta," said her mother, "stay away from cats."

"I will," said Henrietta. The story had scared her.

"Henrietta," said her father, a note of annoyance in his voice, "why can't you complete your work at school?"

"I'm sorry," said Henrietta. Her parents had asked her this question before, and her inability to answer it, or change her behavior, was a source of constant friction. She restlessly pushed her hands between the pillows of the couch.

"Sorry won't help you if you get Finished," said her father. He pointed at her with the television remote.

"Oh, Tom," said her mother, grabbing the remote from him. "Don't be so hard."

"Well, she needs to think about it," said her father. "I don't want her driving a garbage truck the rest of her life." He looked down at Henrietta. "Do *you* want to be a garbage truck driver, Henrietta? Is that what you want?"

"No," said Henrietta, staring at the television screen where a magnetic kitchen cabinet door helped a woman lose weight.

"Good," said her father, folding his arms decisively. He turned to the television also, as an animated toothbrush began to dance in a mouth full of happy teeth.

•• ••●

Later, after eating dinner and watching more TV, Henrietta retired to her bedroom, where she typed her homework on her computer and sent it through the school's automated grading program. Henrietta's homework was generally done quickly and with plenty of mistakes because she didn't proofread.

As she worked, a thought occurred to her. The boy from the bus—what was his name? Gary. With a few keystrokes, she opened the school network. Every student at school had a public page that summarized their performance, which was intended to foster healthy competition.

When Henrietta reached the network's front page, she saw two RedAlerts at the top, and stopped to read them:

REDALERT ONE
AN ISSUE OF DISOBEDIENCE ON A SCHOOL BUS HAS NECESSITATED A CHANGE OF SAFETY HARNESS PROTOCOL. BEGINNING TOMORROW, AUGUST 26, STUDENTS WILL NO LONGER HAVE AUTHORIZATION TO UNBUCKLE THEIR SAFETY HARNESSES UNLESS THE VEHICLE IS IN A FULLY STOPPED POSITION.

Henrietta knew this change had come because of Gary unbuckling his straps. He'd revealed a flaw in the system—that was interesting. She went on to read the next alert:

REDALERT TWO
BEGINNING NEXT WEEK, AUGUST 28, TEXTBOOKS WILL NO LONGER BE USED IN CLASSES. ALL CLASSROOM MATERIALS WILL BE ACCESSED THROUGH THE SCHOOL NETWORK. THIS CHANGE IS FACILITATED THROUGH A PUBLIC-PRIVATE PARTNERSHIP WITH TINCAN TELECOMM: **HELPING SCHOOLS HELP CHILDREN HELP THEMSELVES AND US**™. TEXTBOOKS HAVE MANY DRAWBACKS. THEY CANNOT BE EASILY UPDATED, THEY ARE HEAVY, AND THEY COLLECT MOLD. AS OF THE IMPLEMENTATION DATE, DISPOSE OF ALL TEXTBOOKS IN A SECURE WASTE CONTAINER.

Henrietta looked at her textbook. She wouldn't miss it. It really was pretty heavy.

She clicked around until she found Gary's network page, with his picture at the top. When she saw his performance ratings, her eyes widened. He was number one in the whole class for both reading and math. His behavior on the bus hadn't been suggestive of great intelligence, but there was no arguing with the statistics. Gary was as high up as she was far down. They were opposites.

●·· ··●

At the end of the evening, her mother arrived to tuck her in. She supervised as Henrietta donned her bedclothes, brushed her teeth, and got into bed. She pulled the warm blankets up around Henrietta's ears.

"Did you see the alerts on the school page?" her mother asked.

"Yes," said Henrietta. "Actually, I saw why, with the seat belts."

"What do you mean?"

"A boy unbuckled his, and the bus stopped right in traffic!"

Her mom winced. "Why would he do that? Senseless." She shook her head.

"I don't know," said Henrietta. But maybe she did know. Maybe Gary had just been fed up.

"Stay away from that boy. Do you know his name?" said her mother.

"No," said Henrietta. She didn't often lie to her mother, but this seemed like an unusual case. She was curious about Gary, and didn't want to be forbidden from finding out more.

"I'll just check the BedCam quickly," said her mother, stepping over to the wall, where a small camera was mounted, aimed at Henrietta's bed. The BedCam relayed an image to her parents' room so they could keep an eye on Henrietta during the night. Her mother checked the operations light on the underside of the small unit, and looked at the tiny screen on the back. She frowned.

"What is it, Mom?"

"Henrietta, could you wave at the camera?"

Henrietta waved. Her mother knitted her eyebrows. "I'm going to check this. Keep waving." Her mother stepped from the room. She heard her call her father.

"Just now?" said her father.

Henrietta wondered what was going on as she waved at the blank eye of the lens. Soon her parents entered her bedroom again and her father inspected the camera, pressing some of the buttons on its back in various combinations.

"What's happening?" said Henrietta, finally putting her hand down.

Her mother tried to find words for a moment, and then said, "Come look."

She led Henrietta into the master bedroom, which was considerably larger than Henrietta's and featured a wraparound countertop on which sat two computers, two televisions, and countless cell phones plugged into chargers. (Henrietta's father worked for the communications company TinCan TeleComm, so he always had the latest models.)

Also on the countertop was a video screen plugged directly into the output of the live feed from the BedCam. Henrietta looked at the monitor. There on the screen she saw . . . *herself*, in bed, sleeping. But she wasn't in bed. She was standing right here.

"Is it a recording from last night?" she said.

"It isn't built to record," said Henrietta's father's voice through the wall from her room. "It's a glitch." Henrietta looked at the image of herself on the screen. It was still, like a photo. She was lying on her side, facing the camera, her eyes closed in sleep.

Henrietta and her mother returned to Henrietta's room, and Henrietta looked at the small screen on the camera itself, which showed the same image. After more fruitless button prodding and empty theorizing, Henrietta's parents gave up.

"We all need to get some rest," said her mother. "I'll call the company tomorrow. Would you like to sleep with us tonight, Henrietta?"

"I think I'll just stay in my room," said Henrietta. "I'll be okay."

"Are you sure?" said her mother.

"I'm sure. I can do it."

"If you need anything," said her mother, "even if you're just scared, knock on our door, or call us." She gestured to Henrietta's cell phone, which was charging on her bedside table.

Henrietta climbed back into bed and pulled the covers up, and her mother turned out the light and closed the door. The room glowed yellow from Henrietta's nightlight, a plastic canary with a large round body. Henrietta watched the dark square of the malfunctioning BedCam and eventually fell asleep.

Gary

She awoke just before her alarm went off, thinking she'd heard a thumping sound somewhere in the house. She listened, but it didn't repeat. She got out of bed and changed drowsily into her school clothes, blue pants and a red shirt with a yellow stripe down the back, designed for good visibility. Her room was lit dimly by her nightlight and her computer screen saver. The screen saver was a counting program. At the moment, it was displaying the number 36,548. When it reached 50,000 (in about a month), the computer would shut down and her parents would replace it.

From the other side of the wall, she heard her parents getting up. They were talking, and although the noise was muffled by the wall, Henrietta understood some of the conversation.

". . . afford to stay if the other houses keep getting bigger," said her mother.

"We've been over that," said her father.

"Maybe it's for the best. Get out of this place. Henrietta's House Sickness—"

"It's pointless. We're stuck. And we don't know it's the house's fault, anyway. It could all be for nothing."

Their voices faded as they left the bedroom and moved down the hall into the kitchen.

●·· ··●

After eating breakfast and saying good-bye to her mother, Henrietta walked to the bus stop. The swirls of scented car exhaust dragged at her tired feet. When she reached the crosswalk, she pushed the button and waited for the picture of the dead pedestrian to turn into the picture of the scared pedestrian.

She arrived to find Gary, dressed in matching tan vinyl pants and coat, already there. He was hunched over, kneeling in the artificial turf as she approached, and his short black hair was combed back, plastered to his head and shining. He appeared to be disentangling a piece of trash from where it had become ensnared in the plastic grass blades, muttering to himself under his breath.

When he saw Henrietta approaching, he stood up quickly, looking a little embarrassed. His big eyes were bright black under his thick, black eyebrows, which were the kind that met in the middle. Henrietta didn't speak to him. She felt a little shy and stood a few feet away, watching for the school bus along the line of cars that faded into the hazy distance.

"I'm sorry I was a jerk yesterday!" said Gary loudly. He said it with such drama; it was obvious he'd rehearsed it.

"You were a jerk," said Henrietta. "But I'm sorry you got in trouble."

"Me too." Gary knitted his connected eyebrows for a moment, which made them resemble an inchworm.

"Were your parents mad?" said Henrietta.

"My mom was furious."

"Well, detention is no big deal. I get it almost every day. Oh, did I see you go in the new house yesterday? It's right across the street from me."

"We just moved in," said Gary. "Our house from before got demolished, and we had to move. Which house are you in? Are you in the old one?"

"Yes," she said.

"That's what our house was like. My mom hated it, and so did I. I love our new place. It has heated floors! Our old house was always scary, and it made me sick. At night it creaked and kept me awake."

Henrietta was about to tell him about the mysterious *thump* that had awakened her that morning, but Gary interrupted her with another question. "Do you have many friends here?" he asked. "Are there nice kids here?"

"I don't know," said Henrietta. "I'm . . . kind of unlikable, I think."

"Me *too*!" said Gary. He clenched his hands excitedly.

"Well, maybe we'll get along," said Henrietta.

The bus rolled up just then and opened its door. Henrietta and Gary boarded as Honk Ads blared around them. "BE FAST AND ACCURATE WITH TINCAN'S NEW SKIPPING-STONE PHONE!"

Henrietta felt an odd sensation. It reminded her of when one of her headaches went away. It was happiness.

Headaches

That morning the seating arrangement for the remainder of the year was projected on the screen at the front of class. It had been created by integrating high scoring students with low scoring ones in the hope that low scorers would be positively influenced by their proximity to high scorers and improve the class average. Certain studies suggested that this could happen.

As a result of this reshuffling, Henrietta and Gary found themselves seated next to one another—the lowest scoring student and the highest. As everyone found their seats Ms. Span initiated the math session for the day, and a series of problems appeared at the front.

"Be fast and accurate," she said.

The first problem was:

10 + 4 =

Henrietta typed "14," and the next problem appeared:

25 + 13 =

Next to her, Gary grunted, as if physically trying to push through a pile of dirt to get to his answer. It seemed to cost him physically, which was odd, given his excellent grades.

"Good, Hiroki," said Ms. Span, as she watched everyone's progress on her screen.

Henrietta was just about to type "38," when suddenly, she stopped. Her heart skipped a beat as she felt the strange sensation of someone standing next to her. Then the headache appeared.

She instantly forgot what was happening in the classroom as she reached into her pocket for her pill, popped it into her mouth, and swallowed. She clutched the edge of her desk with both hands as the headache grew.

"Are you okay?" said Gary, leaning toward her.

"I'm getting a headache," Henrietta replied. The headache wobbled one way and then another, and then it tipped and fell behind her left eye, which temporarily went blind. The headache was now medium-sized.

"What's going on back there?" said Ms. Span, removing her reading glasses to peer at the back of the room. Henrietta hadn't noticed, but everyone was turned toward her.

"Henrietta has a headache," said Gary.

"She has permission to see the nurse," said Ms. Span. "The rest of you keep working. Don't let her distract you."

The headache was a yellow, pulsing ball. Each pulse got bigger, and she could see its brightness with her otherwise blind left eye. She stood and stumbled down the aisle of desks. As she exited the classroom, Ms. Span logged her out of the test by entering ILLNESS next to her student number. Gary appeared distracted as well, and Ms. Span decided that perhaps it would benefit Henrietta to have a little help. She scrolled to Gary's name and logged him out, too.

"Gary," she said, "please accompany Henrietta to the infirmary."

Gary stood and followed Henrietta out. She seemed entirely oblivious to his presence as she stumbled through the empty hallway past other classrooms to the nurse's office. She tilted her head forward to keep the headache from rolling around in her skull.

The school nurse, Ms. Morse, looked up from her computer as Henrietta and Gary entered. Ms. Morse was a kind, older woman who always seemed sincerely concerned about Henrietta and all the other children who came to her for help. As Henrietta entered, Ms. Morse asked, "How can I help you two?"

"Henrietta has a headache," said Gary.

"How bad is it, Henrietta?" said Ms. Morse.

"Medium," said Henrietta. Ms. Morse led her to a back room that contained several rows of closely spaced cots. Sometimes when Henrietta arrived other students were being treated, usually for turned ankles or bruised elbows, but today there was no one. Henrietta lay face down on the nearest cot, her forehead pressing into the cream-colored plastic pillow.

"Which eye?" said Ms. Morse.

"Left," said Henrietta.

"Should I call your mom?"

"No." Henrietta wanted the questioning to stop. It was distracting, and she needed to concentrate. She tilted her head further forward on the pillow, to try to pin the headache against her blacked-out eye.

"I'll check back," said Ms. Morse, and she left. There was a clatter of keys as she logged Henrietta and Gary into the infirmary.

Henrietta focused on the headache. Of all the abilities she'd acquired in life (walking, speaking, reading, writing) this was her most advanced. Over the past couple years, she'd become aware of every move of her headaches. She studied them with the intensity that a deer studies a mountain lion.

She kept the pulsing ball contained, and eventually it began to subside, shedding its layers. Finally, it melted to nothing.

●··●●

Her vision returned, although the outlines of everything seemed shaky, and that was how Gary appeared. His edges vibrated.

"Hi," he said. He was sitting opposite her on one of the other cots.

"How did you get in?"

"I came with you," he said. "Ms. Morse said I could stay if I was quiet. School's over now, anyway."

"I didn't even notice you," said Henrietta. "Thanks for coming."

"If we'd been reversed, I wouldn't have noticed you, either. I used to get headaches, too. Like yours. As soon as yours started, I recognized it."

"You don't get them anymore?" said Henrietta.

"Not since my mom and I moved out of our old house. My headaches stopped right away. The doctor says it was House Sickness. I bet that's what you've got, too, because of your old house."

"Did they start behind your forehead?" Henrietta was reluctant to believe Gary had the same problem as she.

"You know what?" Gary leaned toward her conspiratorially.

"What?"

"I knew you were getting it before *you* did. I was doing the math problems, and then I thought I noticed someone standing next to you. I turned to look, but no one was there. Then you reached for your pills."

Henrietta shook her head. "That's impossible."

"But I *knew* it," said Gary. "I saw it before you even did anything."

Henrietta shook her head again, but not too hard—she was still a little dizzy. "Who was there?" she said.

"I couldn't tell," said Gary.

"What's really weird," said Henrietta, "is I always feel like someone's there for a second." Henrietta still felt shaky, and she leaned on Gary as they made their way into the hall.

"We have to go back for detention," she said.

"Ms. Span said we could do it tomorrow, since you were sick and I was . . . well, helping out, I guess," said Gary.

As they stepped through the front doors, they immediately saw that something unusual was happening by the turnaround, where a circle of students had formed. At its center, a kindergartner lay on the ground, curled up. Her face, nearly obscured by curly black hair, was screwed into a grimace. Henrietta recognized her as the girl she'd seen in History and Nutrition, who had left the note on the screen.

Henrietta and Gary pushed forward into the ring of students as one of the bus duty supervisors arrived, a large woman named Mason whom all the children were a little afraid of. The bystanders parted at her approach, and she wordlessly plucked the girl from the pavement. "Nothing to see here. Back in your lines," she said, and strode off toward the infirmary.

Gary whispered, "Let's follow." They walked a small distance behind until Mason disappeared inside Ms. Morse's office with the little girl, and then reappeared alone heading back toward the parking lot turnaround.

"Let's ask Ms. Morse," said Henrietta.

Inside, Ms. Morse sat at her computer, typing. "What can I do for you two?" she said.

"We were wondering about that girl," said Henrietta.

"Rose will be all right." Ms. Morse looked quizzically at the two of them. "You all certainly do stick together," she said.

"We all?" said Gary.

"You kids with headaches," said Ms. Morse.

"Rose has a headache?" said Henrietta.

"Can we go sit with her?" asked Gary, glancing at his phone to see how much time they had before the buses came. It would still be a little while.

"I suppose," said Ms. Morse, "but be quiet. She's resting. Her mother is on the way." She led them back to the cots, where Rose lay curled like a baby bird, her eyes squeezed shut in pain. Ms. Morse indicated that Gary and Henrietta should sit on the cot opposite Rose's.

"Is that what I looked like?" whispered Henrietta.

Gary nodded. "Yeah," he said. "I guess it's probably what I looked like, too, when I got them."

Henrietta felt an ache in her heart. At least when the headache was her own, it occupied her to control it. Watching someone else suffer was in some ways worse. She felt Gary's hand on hers, and she firmly grasped his fingers and tried to think positive thoughts.

Eventually, Rose stirred. She opened her eyes.

"Hello," said Henrietta softly.

Rose didn't reply. She appeared disoriented.

"I'm Henrietta." Henrietta pointed to herself.

"I'm Gary," said Gary a little too loudly. "We go to school here."

"We get headaches, too," said Henrietta. "Like yours."

"I'm Rose." The little girl sat up, holding a hand to her head. "I'm all right. It wasn't bad." She looked back and forth between Henrietta and Gary. "You get them too?"

"Gary used to, and I still do," said Henrietta. "It's House Sickness."

"House Sick?" said Rose.

"Do you live in an old house?" Henrietta asked, but Rose didn't answer. She just sat and waited for Henrietta to continue. "Well, um, if you do, sometimes there are poisons that make you sick."

"We should start a *club*," said Gary. "We're like superheroes who can get incredible headaches on command!"

"That's a terrible idea," said Henrietta, laughing.

Rose smiled. "I'll be treasurer," she said.

From outside, the three heard Ms. Morse's voice: "Hello, Mrs. Soldottir. She has some friends with her."

Ms. Morse entered the room with Rose's mother, a willowy woman with straight blond hair and a long, pretty face, whose skin was considerably lighter in shade than her daughter's. She wore old-fashioned gray pants and a white button-up dress shirt. She was a little out of breath, as if she'd just been running.

"Hi, Mom," said Rose.

"How are you, Rosie?" said her mother, bending and kissing Rose on the forehead.

"I'm okay."

The two of them hugged.

"Were you two helping her?" her mother asked Gary and Henrietta. Henrietta nodded. "Thank you," she said, and her voice contained none of the suspicion or curtness that Henrietta would have expected from either of her own parents, had they been addressing a stranger. "The buses are here. You two should hurry."

The Red Drip

Henrietta sat before her computer that evening, but couldn't concentrate on her homework. There was a lot going on that seemed more important than math. She thought about Gary and Rose, and the headaches they all shared. Until today, she'd felt alone. "House Sickness," she mumbled to herself, her hands hanging motionless above her keyboard. She didn't feel satisfied with that explanation, and her doubts surprised her—normally, she accepted what she was told, but this just didn't add up. She looked around her room. If it was the house's fault, why did she never get sick here?

She recalled Gary's claim that he'd seen someone standing next to her at the onset of her headache that day. She, too, had sensed someone. Rather than "House Sickness," it felt to Henrietta like "Outside Sickness," as if something was waiting for them out there.

She surveyed her small room, its bland white walls, bed, and desk. She always complained about the place, but in fact, she felt safe here. She returned to her homework for a few moments, typing out "I will tread water until help arrives," and "It is never too early to buy life insurance."

On the other side of the wall, her parents had begun arguing.

The voices stopped eventually, and her mother entered, looking careworn.

"Don't forget we're going to your grandmother's tomorrow," she said. "Set your alarm."

"I will."

"And wear your dress shoes."

"I will." Her uncomfortable black plastic dress shoes were already set out by the bedside table.

"Put your pajamas on, brush your teeth, and go to bed," said her mother. Henrietta wouldn't get tucked in tonight.

"Is the BedCam fixed?" said Henrietta, motioning toward the wall where the black BedCam she used to have had been replaced by a new gray one. Her mother frowned.

"They tried three different models, and all of them had the same problem. We'll get it straightened out. Now, pack up your homework." Her mother disappeared into the hallway, and through the wall Henrietta heard her enter the bedroom again.

●·· ··●

Henrietta was named after her grandmother, who was nicknamed Henrie. Henrietta didn't see Grandmother Henrie often, and when she did, the visit was generally short and awkward. Henrietta had always wondered how she ended up with her grandmother's name, because her mother and her grandmother didn't get along very well. If you didn't like your mother, would you name your daughter after her? It made Henrietta wonder if things had been different before she was born.

After thinking on these matters for a few moments, Henrietta's attention drifted back to her textbook. She gazed down at the addition problem she'd been preparing to work out.

It looked . . . strange.

One of the numbers had become a small, perfectly round, red dot.

Henrietta reached out and touched it. It was wet. A little of it came off on her finger. She sniffed it, and the rich smell reminded her of when she skinned her knee once.

It was blood.

She wiped her finger on her pants and checked to see if she was getting a bloody nose, which she wasn't. She stared at the drop. It must have come from somewhere.

She looked up. Above her, emblazoned brightly upon the dingy white ceiling, was a shiny red spot.

Slowly and carefully, Henrietta climbed onto her desk. The drip was seeping through the ceiling along a thin, almost invisible seam. Past the leak, Henrietta followed the seam and saw that it formed a three foot by three foot square. It was a trapdoor.

She visualized her house. She'd never thought about it before, but the pitched roof meant that there was a space, an attic, right over her room. Her first thought was to go to her parents and tell them, but she didn't move. Her mind was racing, and the conclusion to which it sped was that she would not go to them. She stepped down from her desk.

She would look into this herself, right now. From her nightstand, she plucked the flashlight she was supposed to use if there was ever a power outage. Then she climbed back onto the desk.

She pressed gently on the door, and the seam became a dark crack as it tilted upward. She tried to shine her flashlight into the space, but the angle was wrong and her head wasn't high enough to see. She let the door back down, climbed off the desk again, and sat on the edge of her bed. Her heart raced.

It might seem a bit odd that Henrietta, who had been raised to pay such careful attention to safety and the making of sensible decisions, would do something as decidedly unsafe and incautious as investigate something like this alone. It seemed odd to Henrietta, too, and she tried for a moment to convince herself to tell her parents, but she continued to sit, unmoving. She was discovering something about herself that she'd not known before. She was discovering that she was an intensely curious person.

After a few moments she stood, picked up her chair, and placed it quietly on top of her desk. Then she climbed on, balancing precariously, and crouched against the ceiling. She put one hand against the door, knitted her eyebrows, counted to three . . . and stood up.

●·· ··●

The attic was larger than she'd imagined. A bank of tall windows to the left admitted the pale light of a greenish full moon, lighting what seemed to be a little living room immediately before her containing a low coffee table with a glass top, a sofa upholstered with a faded flower print, a small end table with a hardcover dictionary placed atop, and two wicker chairs. Behind this stood many tall, full bookcases, which largely blocked the view further into the attic, but Henrietta could see the space stretching back behind them into the shadows, moonbeams glancing upon many obscure, still shapes. Overhead, the peaked rafters diminished into the darkness.

Henrietta was so overwhelmed by it all that for a moment she scarcely noticed what lay immediately before her. When her gaze finally dropped down, she gasped and lunged back against the edge of the door, wobbling uncertainly on the chair atop her desk.

An enormous gray cat lay there, in a puddle of blood.

Ms. Span's voice popped into Henrietta's head instantly, warning her about the risk of bodily fluids, infection, tetanus, dust mites, rabid animals, and falling from heights. But Henrietta didn't budge.

The cat seemed unconscious. Additionally, it wasn't really a cat. It was twice as large as an ordinary housecat. One of its hind legs was splayed out behind its body, as long and thin as a stilt, like nothing Henrietta had ever seen.

She hoisted herself the rest of the way into the attic, keeping a safe distance. The cat's tall ears twitched, and it opened its eyes, which shone in the moonlight an incandescent emerald green with wide, black pupils.

"Hello," Henrietta whispered breathlessly.

The cat didn't make any threatening moves. Henrietta turned on her flashlight. Her eyes were drawn to a patch of wet, matted fur on the cat's hindquarter, where blood pulsed out, thick and slow. She thought back to Physical Safety period at school. This was an arterial wound.

"APPLY DIRECT PRESSURE TO ARTERIAL WOUNDS FOR FIVE MINUTES," she whispered to herself. "Please don't scratch me, kitty." She reached into her pocket and pulled out her cell phone to mark the five-minute interval, but the screen was blank. She shook it, but nothing changed. She removed her sweater, wrapped it around her hand and forearm for protection, and pressed on the gash. The cat's breathing quickened, but to Henrietta's relief it didn't lash out.

She counted out the full five minutes, then slowly removed her hand. Under the matted gray hair, the bleeding seemed to have slowed.

"I'm going to get some things to help you," she said. "Don't go anywhere."

She descended carefully back into her room and tiptoed out into the hallway. As she passed the master bedroom, her mother's voice rang out. "Henrietta? Is that you?"

"Um . . . going to the bathroom."

"Then straight to bed."

"Yes, Mom." When she reached the bathroom, she debated what to take from the medicine cabinet. Veterinary science wasn't emphasized at school beyond "INJURED ANIMALS ARE DANGEROUS." But Henrietta did recall an old television show she'd watched once, in which a boy helped an injured horse, shaving the hair from the wound and bandaging it. Henrietta selected one of her father's safety razors, a bottle of hydrogen peroxide, a package of sterile gauze pads, a tube of antibacterial ointment, and a roll of medical tape.

She headed back along the hallway, but as she passed her parents' bedroom, her mother's voice stopped her again.

"*Henrietta*," it said curtly.

"Yes?" said Henrietta, pausing in the hall, trying not to drop any of her supplies.

"You forgot to flush."

"Oh, right!" She quickly returned to the bathroom, flushed the toilet, and headed toward her room again.

"Straight to bed now," said her mother's voice. "And don't forget to set your alarm."

"I won't forget!" said Henrietta, hurrying past.

It was strange to enter her bedroom and see the dark square hole in her ceiling. Two minutes away from it had nearly convinced her it wasn't real. Once again, she entered the greenish glow of the moonlit attic.

The cat remained as she had left it, watching her with its enormous green eyes. Once Henrietta was inside this time, she shut the attic door behind her.

She laid out her supplies in front of the cat. "I'm going to try to help you with these," she said. Hesitantly, she began. She put her hands gently on the cat, and examined the wound. It was tough to see through the fur, and she began to shave carefully. The cat shivered as the blade touched its skin, but Henrietta successfully cleared the wound. It was small, but there was no telling how deep. It looked like a stab. Thick, dark blood pulsed out slowly.

Henrietta applied hydrogen peroxide and antibacterial ointment, and covered the wound with a piece of gauze, which she affixed with medical tape. The cat's tense breathing slowed as she finished.

"I hope it's okay," she whispered. "I have to go. I'll come back tomorrow if I can."

She took one last glance around the attic. The angled walls of exposed rafters glowed in the moonlight, and deep in the space, beyond the bookshelves, stretched a fascinating maze of dim sights: stacked furniture, sealed trunks, towers of boxes.

Reluctantly, she lowered herself into her room and pulled the trapdoor closed. It sealed up as perfectly as ever, leaving only the dot of blood at the edge, which Henrietta wiped away with the arm of her sweater.

In bed, she stared at the ceiling and imagined the animal that was right above her, sitting in the moonlit shadows of the most mysterious place she'd ever seen. And suddenly something occurred to her: when she was in the attic, no one had known she was there. She had been alone.

Sunset

hirp. The sound came from her cell phone. She'd overslept! When she answered the call, her mother's voice sounded simultaneously over the speaker and through the house from the kitchen. "Henrietta!"

"Sorry!" said Henrietta.

"Hurry up!"

"I'm hurrying." Henrietta rushed into the hallway to find her mother already there. She gasped when she saw her daughter.

"Sweetie!" She reached out and took Henrietta's hand, which was covered in rust-red dried blood. She'd forgotten to wash it off.

She jerked back. "I . . . cut myself," she said. "Picking glass out of my shoe."

"We have to clean it," said her mother, "and bandage it. Let me—"

"I'll do it after I shower. We're late." Henrietta slipped past her mother and closed the door on her. She stepped into the shower, trying to gather her thoughts. Trapdoor. Cat. She looked at the red-brown flakes on her hand. She had really done all of that. "Make it quick!" said her mother from outside— she was already in the bad mood that always possessed her when they visited Henrietta's grandmother and Al. Henrietta's mother had never liked Al for some reason that Henrietta couldn't fathom. To Henrietta, he just seemed like a nice old man, but her mother had been enraged when he and Grandmother Henrie had married two years ago, and since then Henrietta barely ever saw them.

After her shower, Henrietta found her clothes laid out: a long-sleeved shirt printed with yellow leaves, dark green pants, and her dreaded black plastic formal shoes. She threw everything on, and only remembered at the last moment the cut she'd lied about. She went to the medicine cabinet and wrapped a bandage around her thumb.

Because visits to her grandmother's often involved her sitting in a corner somewhere with nothing to do, she grabbed her textbook from her desk as she walked out, hoping she might study a little. She glanced regretfully up at the trapdoor as she left, wishing in vain for a moment to rush up there and check on the cat.

●··●●

When Henrie and Al married two years ago, they'd moved together to Sunset Estates, a retirement community far out in the Addition, which was an hour's drive out across the endless traffic jam. Along the way they passed Henrietta's school. Henrietta looked at the long, low buildings and wished she was there, which was something she'd never wished before. But she had two friends now, and an amazing story to tell them when she saw them next.

"TURN LEFT AT THE INTERSECTION," suggested the friendly voice of the car's computer. Henrietta's father entered the turn lane.

"What are you smiling about back there?" he said, unexpectedly. Henrietta's eyes snapped into focus. He was watching her in the rearview mirror.

"Nothing," she said. She was a bit shy of her father, partly because she didn't see much of him. He often worked late during the week, and sometimes even on the weekend.

"Are you dreaming about a boy?" he asked impishly, raising one eyebrow to show he wasn't completely serious. But he wasn't completely unserious either.

"No," said Henrietta. She wrinkled her nose as if to say, *yuck*.

"Leave her alone, Tom," said her mother.

"We're just joking," said her father.

"It's embarrassing her."

"No it isn't." Her father's voice lost its levity. Just then, his cell phone rang. Henrietta's father's cell phone was a small, flat oval resembling a polished stone. No one else had anything like it, but her father's employer, TinCan TeleComm, always gave him the latest models early. TinCan was a new company that had formed recently when two other companies merged. Her father's job, as far as Henrietta understood it, was to help the new company communicate with itself. He'd tried once or twice to explain further, with limited success. At the moment, he listened to his polished egg, and then spouted off a string of information Henrietta could scarcely interpret.

"If I.T. can't keep Skipping-Stone's PS for UPC, Marketing just has more time, so it doesn't matter. Right."

"TURN LEFT AT THE NEXT INTERSECTION," said the car's computer. "WHILE YOU DRIVE, WOULD YOU LIKE TO HEAR SOME ADVERTISEMENTS FOR PRODUCTS THAT MIGHT INTEREST YOU?"

"Not right now," said Henrietta's mother.

"I.T. thinks that's important, but it isn't," said Henrietta's father. "Tell them it doesn't matter." This was often what her father said on business calls. Telling people what didn't matter, Henrietta thought, seemed to matter.

The phone conversation continued, as did the directions from the car's computer, until the sign for Sunset Estates appeared:

The car turned into the mazelike complex, composed of single-level row houses with tan vinyl exteriors. Each house was identical to the next, resulting in a pattern as they drove: Garage, porch, front door. Garage, porch, front door. Traffic was considerably less here—it was one of the only places in the Addition where cars were sparse, because it was a dead end.

Henrietta's father concluded his conversation, returned his phone to his pocket, and looked at Henrietta again in the rearview mirror. "Now, about that boyfriend," he said, smiling.

"His name's Gary," said Henrietta, suddenly curious to see what such an admission would bring about.

"*Who?*" said her mother, turning around and gripping the headrest of her seat with one hand. She had painted her fingernails for the birthday party, and they shone bright pink.

"I knew it!" said her father, triumphantly. He banged one hand on the steering wheel, as if to affix his astuteness there for display.

"He's my friend, not my *boy*friend," said Henrietta. "He's the best student in our class, actually."

"The highest rank?" said her mother. "That boy Gary?"

"Yes."

"That's wonderful, Henrietta! Maybe he could help you on your homework. It's good to make good friends."

"And you never know, love *could* blossom," her father jibed.

"Stop it," said her mother, still not amused.

"ARRIVING AT ZERO FIVE, ZERO SEVEN, SIX THREE TWO," said the computer.

"Zero five, zero seven, six three two," said Henrietta to herself, for no particular reason. *If you repeat it a few times, you'll remember it*, she reflected. Just like the composition sentences at school that stuck in her head, or certain Honk Ads she heard over and over.

Henrietta's father parked, and they exited the car. Henrietta tucked her textbook under one arm and they approached the front door of a home that looked like all the rest, except for its unique address: 0507-632. Henrietta's dress shoes pinched, and she walked strangely, trying to find a way to proceed that didn't hurt too much.

Henrietta's father rang the bell, commencing a computer-generated rendition of "Jingle Bells," and the door opened. There stood Al, a smile lighting his old face. Al was a stooped gentleman, skinny as a stick, wearing black slacks and a green cardigan. Behind him, Henrietta could see and hear the party—guests talking and laughing, holding drinks, sitting or standing. All of them were old.

"Hello, kids!" said Al boisterously, his old voice crackling. "I saw you through the window. It's been too long!" He briskly shook Henrietta's father's hand, saying, "Young Tom!" He hugged Henrietta's mother. "Good to see you, Aline." Then he looked down at Henrietta.

"Henrietta! What occupies your thoughts these days?"

"Oh," said Henrietta, thrown off guard by a real question. Al seemed to sense her discomfort.

"Do you accept hugs or handshakes, young lady?" he asked.

"Handshakes," said Henrietta.

"She accepts *hugs*, of course," said Henrietta's mother, a note of annoyance in her voice. She prodded Henrietta slightly from behind. It was odd—Henrietta knew she didn't like Al, but for some reason still felt it necessary for Henrietta to hug him.

Al, however, quickly held out his hand, and Henrietta shook it. "I watched you on the porch," he said genially, "and I got the impression your shoes were a little uncomfortable. Am I right?"

"They're super uncomfortable," said Henrietta.

"You know how I could tell? Because you walked like *this*!" said Al, and he limped comically ahead of the three of them, waving for them to accompany him through the crowd. Henrietta's father laughed, a laugh Henrietta recognized as fake, and the three of them followed Al inside.

The house was packed with all kinds of people united by the bonds of their common oldness. In her daily life, Henrietta saw very few old people, and it was daunting to encounter so many at once. Of course, the reason she didn't see many elderly people was because they all lived in Sunset Estates and other similar communities.

Through a sliding glass door on the opposite side of the living room drifted sizzling sounds and the rich, charred smells of a barbecue. Henrietta's mother would never allow an open flame near their house, and barbecue skewers could cause terrible accidents. But there it was, a metal clamshell on the rear patio, tongues of orange flame cooking steaks, hot dogs, and kebabs in sizzling rows. It was so mesmerizing that Henrietta didn't notice she was standing right next to her grandmother until she looked up to see Al, Henrie, and both of her parents watching her.

"Say *hello*, Henrietta," said her father, a little sharply.

"Would you like a handshake or a hug, Henrietta?" said her grandmother, a short, elderly woman with a pronounced stoop. Henrietta looked up at her and suddenly noted the family resemblance between her grandmother, her mother, and herself, all three of them women with ruddy skin, blockish features, and sturdy frames. This was not, at the moment, a pleasant realization—Henrietta felt strangely trapped by it.

"A handshake," said Henrietta determinedly, though she could feel her mother's withering gaze. She held out her hand, and briefly grasped her grandmother's cool, papery fingers.

They sat with Henrie on a soft, cream-colored couch in the living room. Henrietta thought her grandmother looked tired. In fact, there was something of a forced gaiety to everyone at the party.

●· · ··●

The morning melted into a series of loosely connected vignettes of dodging around long legs and overhearing snippets of conversations until the barbecue was ready, and everyone ate. Henrietta was starved because she'd missed breakfast, and she gulped her food ravenously. It tasted excellent, especially the charred bits.

"Don't eat the charred bits," said her mother.

As they all finished their meal, Al turned to Henrietta. "So, Henrietta," he said, "I've heard you're interested in reading."

"Yes, I like reading," she said, though she wondered where Al would have heard about it.

"I've got a few old books in the basement you might enjoy," he said. "You do know what a book is, don't you?" He smiled.

Henrietta held up her textbook silently as an example, a little defensive over being poked fun at.

"Be careful on the stairs," said her father.

"If the books are moldy, hold your breath," said her mother.

"Walk *this* way!" said Al. As he limped forward, again mocking Henrietta's gait in her uncomfortable shoes, he shot a significant glance at Henrie that terminated in an inscrutable wink.

This time Henrietta imitated his walk, and doing so helped her avoid the pinchiest parts of her shoes. The two of them clowned through a crowded hallway to a narrow white vinyl door where several people lingered in conversation.

"Excuse us," said Al, "we're walking *this way*." He limped through the crowd, opened the door, and headed down a dark, carpeted staircase. Henrietta followed.

A few steps in, Al flipped a light switch, illuminating a series of overhead fluorescent panels. Henrietta had imagined the basement would be like the attic in her house—old, shadowy, and full of cobwebs. But this house was built recently, and its basement was a regular room, full of the stinging scent of new carpet.

Henrietta closed the door behind, but didn't let the latch click shut, remembering Ms. Span's lectures about getting trapped in basements, car trunks, and refrigerators, all of which would result first in suffocation, followed quickly by dehydration, hypothermia, and finally starvation (in that order).

Al descended the stairs slowly, leaning a little on the tan handrail. At the bottom, several plastic folding chairs surrounded a small, vinyl-topped card table. The basement was about the size of the living room upstairs, but instead of being full of people, it was full of books, stacked on shelves and in cases.

"Everything down here is plastic, except the books," said Al as he and Henrietta sat at the table. "These shelves are actually part of the house. It's one molded piece." He gestured to where the tan shelves merged seamlessly with the wall.

On the table before them lay two books, which Al had obviously placed with the intent of showing to Henrietta. "All of the books down here are Henrie's and my collection, which we combined when we moved in together. These two are interesting—one was mine, and one was Henrie's. Can you tell which is older?" he asked.

Both books looked old, and the writing on their covers was a highly ornamented cursive that was difficult to read.

"They have the same title," Henrietta observed.

"They're different editions of the same thing. Look at this one from the side. See how thick it is? Compare." One was considerably thicker than the other. "What do you think?"

"One has more pages."

"If you wrote a book about something, and then wrote it again a few years later, would the new one be shorter?"

"Longer," said Henrietta. "I'd know more."

"Just so," Al said. He opened each book to a random page. "Now look inside, and tell me the difference."

"One is typed, and one is . . . handwriting?" said Henrietta.

"The older one is handwriting. It's so old, they hadn't invented typing yet. The thicker book, the newer one, is typed." Al closed both books, and Henrietta studied the title on their covers, trying to untangle the cursive. "It's fascinating, isn't it, to see how people figure out things? How they learn, and fill more books."

"So, is mine the best of all?" said Henrietta, holding up her textbook.

"What do *you* think?" said Al. Henrietta looked at the shiny, plastic cover. "I like yours," she said.

"Why?"

"They're just . . . interesting. The handwritten one most of all."

"That's nice to hear," said Al. He smiled. "It's good for an old person like me to know that young people like old things. Look at the title a little more. Have you ever seen cursive?"

"A little," said Henrietta. "B-e-s . . . the word is . . . Bestiary?" She pronounced it BEST-ee-airy.

"That's right," said Al. "But it's pronounced BEAST-ee-airy. Do you know it?"

"No," said Henrietta.

"Say 'not yet,' when someone asks you that," said Al. He winked.

"You winked at Grandma Henrie when we left the living room."

"I'm a winker," said Al.

Henrietta tried to wink in response, but she blinked instead. "Were you sharing a secret?"

"You're an observant girl," said Al. "Henrie and I have a few secrets, some that we've kept a long time. Most haven't been worth it. Do you think that's true?"

"I don't know," said Henrietta. "Some secrets might be important." She thought about the secret hiding in her attic back home.

"Perhaps," said Al. He paused. "Your grandmother asked me to take you down here so she could talk to your parents. She's going to tell them something they won't want you to hear." Henrietta didn't respond. She could tell Al was going to say more. "Henrietta, your grandmother has cancer. She's going to die."

Henrietta suddenly felt very uncomfortable, and she found her eyes drawn to the two old books, covers facing up, resting before Al on the table. The ornate calligraphy was metallic gold.

"This party isn't just a birthday party," Al continued. "It's a farewell party."

"I thought it seemed sad," said Henrietta.

"Your grandmother is eighty today," said Al. "You might not be able to imagine how old that is, but I'll tell you—it's the blink of an eye. That's as old as anyone ever gets."

"I don't know what to say," said Henrietta.

"Say anything or nothing," said Al. "The important thing is that you know. You don't need to be protected from it." A drop of water appeared suddenly right in the middle of the older book's cover. It was a perfect circle, and it came from nowhere. Henrietta thought of the drop of blood she'd seen the night before, and she looked up at the ceiling. She'd once watched a TV news story about a family who drowned when their basement flooded. She looked at Al to see if he'd noticed it.

He was crying. He wiped his eyes with one old hand.

"I don't know grandma very well," said Henrietta. This was difficult for her to admit for some reason, and it felt bad to say.

"Your parents don't come over much," said Al. "It isn't your fault, Henrietta. In fact, if it's anyone's, it's mine."

"Yours?" Henrietta looked curiously into Al's tear-reddened eyes.

He smiled. "It's a strange world," he said.

"I know." Henrietta nodded. In fact, she felt she'd only learned of the world's strangeness recently.

"I assume you're aware that your mother was against Henrie's and my marriage."

Henrietta had never been expressly told, but she'd certainly heard her parents talking about it plenty of times. "Yes," she said.

"Do you know much about your grandfather?" Al asked.

"Mom said he got sick from his work, and died."

"His name was Roy," said Al. "He and I were friends. In fact, I was his best man when he married your grandmother. Did you know that?"

Henrietta shook her head. With regard to this subject, she knew pretty much nothing, but she had long been curious.

"Roy was an agrichemical scientist, and he did grow ill from it. He was bedridden for the better part of two years before he died, and I tried to help him and your grandmother. I was at their house almost every day, tending to your grandfather's needs and helping keep the house in order. Your mother was about your age, then. And, we didn't plan it, Henrietta, but . . . well, your grandmother and I fell in love during that time." Al paused, and picked up the older *Bestiary* and turned it restlessly in his hands.

"Your mother sensed what was happening, I believe. When Roy died, I think she blamed your grandmother and me. And maybe she was right. Henrie and I tried to end our relationship. We stopped seeing each other. We hoped we'd fall out of love. But we didn't—we couldn't. Even as the years passed. So, once Aline was out on her own and had started her own family, we faced our feelings. I asked Henrie to marry me. You know the rest—we moved out here together, and you and your parents moved into her old house."

"We didn't go to the wedding," said Henrietta.

Al shook his head, studying the book in his hands. "I wish things had been otherwise," he said. Then he suddenly looked up and met Henrietta's gaze and held it. "You know what?" he said. "Maybe they still can be otherwise, Henrietta. After all, we aren't dead yet!" He put the book decisively down on the table with a thump. "Henrietta, by gosh, let me ask you something. I'd like to be your grandfather. What do you think? Do you want a grandfather? Some silly old man?"

Henrietta hesitated. Al was, after all, more or less a stranger to her. She knew her mother disliked him, which made her feel uncomfortable. But at the same time, she saw him clearly—sitting there, his hands clasped nervously on the tabletop, worried she'd reject him. When you yourself are rejected almost every day, it becomes easy to spot in the faces of other people. And perhaps that's one good thing about rejection—it allows you to help others, if you choose to.

"You're not a silly old man," Henrietta said. She looked him up and down, joking a little as if she were studying a product for sale in a store. "I think you'll make a good grandfather," she said.

Al smiled, and released the breath he'd been holding. "Hey," he said, "I haven't given you the tour down here yet." He stood and gestured to Henrietta to follow him, and they walked back among the plastic bookcases. Al pointed out a few volumes as they passed. "There's an old journal—probably my oldest book. And that one's called *How To*—it has all kinds of instructions in it, like how to build a bird house."

"I saw a bird once," said Henrietta. As she looked at the hundreds, maybe thousands, of titles she thought about how computers had made books obsolete. Even her own textbook, which was practically brand new, was outdated.

On the far wall of the room, past the last set of tall shelves, stood a narrow sliding door. Al pulled it open. "This is the only other room down here. I keep my tools in it. It's pretty jammed full."

The little room was lit with fluorescent lights just like the main room, and the walls were lined with more plastic shelves, which were crowded with old tools instead of old books. Henrietta recognized some of them: a skill saw, a few hammers with different heads, drills, wrenches.

"Have you ever seen tools?" Al asked.

"In safety videos," said Henrietta. "They're dangerous. We don't have any."

"Everything just snaps together nowadays, but there was a time when people had to build from scratch. I keep these back here thinking they'll eventually come in handy."

"You're nostalgic," said Henrietta. She'd seen a movie in class where a father kept some tools out of nostalgia, but then his son died when a hammer fell on him.

"Guilty as charged!" said Al, laughing. He closed up the tool room, and they returned to the card table and plastic chairs by the staircase. Henrietta's mind was carefully circling everything she and Al had talked about. Her eyes played over the covers of the two bestiaries on the table: one ancient and slim, the other old and thick. If people were books, she thought, she'd added a few chapters to herself in the last twelve hours. Finally, she spoke. "I have a secret to tell you, Al," she said.

Al looked at her seriously, and took a seat at the table. "I'm honored to hear it, Henrietta," he said.

Henrietta reached out to the older of the two books, and opened the cover a crack. "I found an attic above my room," she said. "It's full of stuff. And . . . a cat. It was bleeding, and I tried to help it."

Al leaned toward her as Henrietta lowered the cover of the book.

"What did it look like?" he asked.

"Actually, it's not really like a cat," said Henrietta.

"Did it have long legs?" said Al. He held out his hands to indicate roughly how long he meant. "Big green eyes?"

Henrietta was so surprised that it took her a moment to stammer, "Yes!"

"Henrietta," Al said, leaning forward even more, "you've made an *amazing* discovery. The cat in your attic is a wild housecat!"

Al's excitement was catching. Henrietta felt her heart beat faster. "I don't know what that is," she said, leaning forward a little bit herself. She and Al looked like a pair of conspirators.

"You've heard of domestic housecats," said Al. "They're just like domestic horses, or domestic dogs—they've lived with people so long, they've become used to us. But all of those domestic animals have wild ancestors—wild horses and wild dogs. The same is true of housecats. There are domestic housecats and wild housecats. Now, wild animals are very strange creatures. They don't have anything to do with people. Have you ever seen a wild horse, or a wild dog? Maybe on TV?"

"On history shows," said Henrietta.

"They're all extinct now," said Al. "People made so many buildings and roads that those animals had nowhere left to live. They died out."

"But where do wild housecats live?" said Henrietta.

"In houses," said Al, "that's why they're called housecats. Normally they lived in basements or attics, but the old homes they needed have all been torn down now, except a few. The new plastic houses, like this one, are no good—the cats can't get into them. Also, people misunderstood them, and thought they were dangerous."

"I've heard cats are dangerous."

"Everything is dangerous," said Al, "but not everything is *particularly* dangerous." He paused. "Henrietta, I'm proud of you. What you did was very brave.

And you were smart to keep it a secret. If your parents knew, they'd probably have the cat exterminated."

"Some secrets *are* worth keeping," said Henrietta.

Al smiled. "Now, as for the rest of what's in that attic—"

Before he could finish, the basement door opened, and Henrietta's mother stuck her head in at the top of the stairwell. "Henrietta," she said, her scowling face hovering over the white ruffles of her blouse. "We're leaving. Now. Your father is in the car."

"All right," said Henrietta. Her mother removed herself and shut the door. Henrietta turned to Al. "The attic," she said.

"Those things belonged to Henrie," said Al, standing. "I wonder if Henrie even remembers it's all up there—inventory from her old store." As Al fell silent, he picked up the older of the two bestiaries from the tabletop. "Henrietta, let me quickly show you this a little more." He opened it. "See how the edges of the pages are dusted in gold? And how the paper is sewn into the binding, and the hand-colored inside cover? Now, if your parents ask, you can tell them what we talked about." He winked at her. "It's a funny coincidence that I pulled these down, actually. When you learn the word *bestiary*, you'll understand why I decided to give you this." He held out the older of the two editions. "I hope it provides you with good information."

Henrietta didn't know what to say. She carefully took the book in her hands. It was heavy and smelled of old paper, leather, and Al's cologne. The binding was rough and dry.

She looked at her own textbook, which sat on the table between the two of them. "Would you like to trade?" she asked.

"I can't take your schoolbook, Henrietta," said Al.

"It isn't my schoolbook anymore. Starting tomorrow we aren't going to use it. Everything will be on computer."

Al took the plastic book in his hands and looked it over. "All right," he said. "I'll consider it a donation. Thank you, Henrietta."

They ascended the carpeted stairs together. When they reached the top, Henrietta pushed on the door, but it didn't give.

"My mom locked us in!" she said, surprised.

Al laughed, and opened his phone. "I guess we should call for help. Unfortunately, cell phones don't work very well down here. I've been meaning to talk to your father about it." He dialed and handed his phone to Henrietta, who put it to her ear. The line was full of static, but soon her grandmother answered: "Al, are you stuck down there again?"

"Hi, Grandma," said Henrietta. "My mom trapped us by accident."

Henrie laughed. "I'll rescue you," she said.

Henrietta and Al listened through the door to the muted din of the party, Henrietta holding her new book in her arms, until the latch clicked and the door opened to reveal Henrie's amused face. She gazed down at Henrietta searchingly, and again Henrietta noticed the similarities between her and her mother.

"She knows," said Al.

"What does she know?" said Henrie.

"I love you, Grandma," said Henrietta. She held out her arms and hugged her grandmother, and Al joined them.

Supplement to the Seventh Edition of the Bestiary
by Aristotle Alcott, Henrift, and Friends

Introduction

This Addendum is published coincident with the release of the
Seventh Edition of the Bestiary, in service to those Readers already in
possession of a copy of our previous, Sixth, Edition. This Addendum
contains only those Entries added or Amended for the Seventh Edition.
Paste this supplement inside the Back Cover of your Bestiary, which
was bound with Great Care to ensure its sufficiency against such
Amalgamations. It is our dearest hope that you find in these Entries both
Utility and Enjoyment. Rest assured we shall continue with each new
Edition to publish simultaneously a Supplement for those whose
Generosity supported our earlier efforts.

Submissions

The Bestiary flourishes in accordance with the Submissions we receive
from Observant Friends! If you should chance upon any Creature as
yet unrecorded herein, or if you survey a new Habit or Detail about
a previously Recorded Creature, please submit, in writing, your
observations. If they should come to Reside between the Covers of a
future Edition, your Name will appear under the designation "Observed
By." Illustrations, likewise, may be included, though we frequently
(and with all Humility having hereby requested and hereafter supposed
your Assent) revise Submissions to ensure a happy continuity of
Style and Aesthetic in this, our Most Humble Enterprise.

Send Submissions to: Aristotle Alcott
The Gerry Oak with The Knuckle
c/o Running Press Book Publishers
2300 Chestnut Street, Philadelphia, PA 19103

small and black,
no feathers

wings transform
from black to red
to yellow of
Deciduous leaves.

Autumn Bat

For the majority of the Year, the Autumn Bat appears as a small, black, featherless, flying nocturnal mammal that roosts in Caves and feeds on Airborne Insects. However, with the arrival of autumn, the Bat's wings transform from black to the reds and yellows of Deciduous Leaves. It forsakes the Caves and roosts instead among the branches of Maple Trees. During this period, the Bats select Mates. With the first frost, their colorful coat returns again to Black, and they resume their familiar Habits.

—Observed and Recorded by A.A.

Airship Whale

Easily the largest Creature in the forest, the Airship Whale is also the lightest. Mature specimens grow to Lengths in excess of a hundred feet, and weigh, as

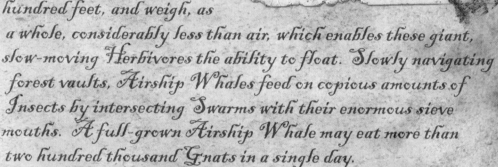

a whole, considerably less than air, which enables these giant, slow-moving Herbivores the ability to float. Slowly navigating forest vaults, Airship Whales feed on copious amounts of Insects by intersecting Swarms with their enormous sieve mouths. A full-grown Airship Whale may eat more than two hundred thousand Gnats in a single day.

The Airship Whale's ability to float was long a mystery, but careful observation of deceased Specimens revealed them to be largely hollow and filled during life with a great deal of superheated air. Thus, while it seems on first sight that the Airship Whale would be of considerable value as a Foodstuff to humans, the want of meat (only the tail and flippers have any useful amount) ensures they are rarely Consumed.

— Commonly observed. Recorded by A.A.

navigated forest — over a hundred feet long

Pif / Paf / Greater Pif

A small Woodpecker feeding primarily on Grubs, the Pif is most often identified by the striking checkerboard pattern of red and white feathers that adorn its Neck, not to be confused with the closely related Paf, whose distinguishing characteristic is a similarly situated Checkerboard of red and black. Interbreeding of Pif and Paf produces the Greater Pif, a bird of considerably larger proportion than either parent, characterized by a Piflike black-and-white checked neck. The Greater Pif has never been observed nesting, and it is assumed to be Infertile.

—Observed by Henrift. Recorded by A.A.

Statium

Considerable debate has surrounded the inclusion of this small, mossy haired Biped in the Bestiary, as it is unclear whether or not it is Alive. As far as it has been observed, the Statium neither Grows, Reproduces, nor Dies. Nonetheless, its stable population continues to rise each day and go about its Mysterious Activities, which include waking up in the Early Morning Hours and wandering about Aimlessly. Once each year the Statia Convene, finding one another through an Unknown Method and standing motionless, in close proximity. After several days of Stillness, they disperse.

One Statia was shot with an arrow by a curious Hunter, and the shot seemed to do it no harm, though the arrow did pierce it, and continues to persist in it to this day, giving it the Common Name of Pierced Statium. Several other Statia have names known locally to those who observe them.

— Commonly observed. Recorded by A.A.

Forest Lion

An exceedingly impressive Mammal, the average male
Forest Lion weighs from three to six hundred pounds
(females two to five hundred). Most easily identified by
its Emerald Green Coat, the Forest Lion prospers in prides
of ten to twenty Individuals, though such Associations
are impermanent, and single Lions often hunt in isolation for
months at a time.

Despite their Prodigious Size, Forest Lions can Disguise
themselves easily due to their Natural Camouflage, and are
considered extremely dangerous, preying upon Humans
with Disturbing Frequency. However, it is important also
to remember that these Lions are an essential part of our
Environment, and should not be wantonly Massacred.

If you are threatened
by a Forest Lion, try to
appear large by holding
out your Arms. Speak
Loudly and throw Rocks.
The Lion has probably
never had anything thrown
at it before, and may
become confused.

— Commonly observed.
Recorded by A.A.

Tail Fox

A strangely extroverted animal, the Tail Fox is often found playing. Adolescent specimens particularly will attempt to coax even Humans into a Carefree Gambol. The Fox's chief goad is its Tail,

adolescent specimen, full-grown tail will grow to twice its length

a magnificent, Fluffy Appendage twice as long as the Fox itself, which is variegated in colors of brown, white, and orange.

Tail Foxes occasionally fall victim to their own Playfulness, and it is not uncommon to find them having harmed themselves in the midst of a Revel. Nonetheless, there must be some Advantage to it, or one would expect to find the Population declining. This uncommonly amusing Animal is generally enjoyed and rarely hunted because of its pleasing demeanor.

— Commonly observed. Recorded by A.A.

Helium Fungus

A Common Fungus that proliferates underground in Cedar Groves, several exceptionally large colonies of Helium Fungus have been discovered, some exceeding a hundred acres in size. Their subterranean Habit frustrates easy Identification, leaving one to speculate that even larger Examples may exist.

The name Helium Fungus arises from this Fungus's peculiar production of Helium Gas during the fruiting period. In the spring and autumn, when the Fruiting Bodies (aka mushrooms) appear, the deep, wide parasols (measuring up to twelve inches in diameter) release and accumulate Helium Gas, finally detaching with their Stalks and floating into the Air to travel for periods of a week or more as they release millions of Spores.

— Commonly observed.
Recorded by A. A.

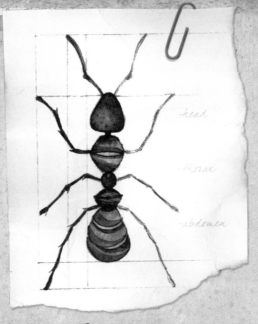

head

thorax

abdomen

Plumb Ant

A frequent occupant of Stumps and fallen Logs, in which it establishes colonies of one- to five-thousand, the Plumb Ant is exceedingly Beneficial to anyone in necessity of reckoning accurate Measurement, due to the perfect equivalence among all Workers of the attributes of Weight, Volume, and Length. Many Professionals maintain Colonies near workshops or laboratories, or purchase jars of twenty-five, fifty, a hundred, or more Plumb Ant Carapaces for use with Scales or Displacement Measurements.

—Observed and Recorded by A.A.

Observed and Recorded by A.A.

Acuteipede/Obtuseipede

The Acutipede and Obtuseipede are separate but similar species of Bent Centipede. The thorax of the Creatures forms a vertex from which two Many-legged Abdomens emerge, forming the lines of an angle of 50/310 degrees. The head emerges from the thorax suchwise as to bisect the acute angle (in the case of the Acuteipede) or the inverse obtuse angle (in the case of the Obtuseipede).

Both species have a Virulently Poisonous bite, but the placement of the Acuteipede's mouth, in the midst of the narrow angle, prevents it from harming Humans. The Obtuseipede, however, can bite Humans, and the Poison is potentially Lethal.

This following Simple Rhyme can aid in recalling which of the two is to be feared:

> If it's acute
> The point is moot.
> If it's obtuse,
> And on the loose,
> Flee.

—Observed by Henrift.
Recorded by A.A. Poem by Henrift.

Tree Goat

A Creature of astounding Gracefulness, the Tree Goat lives almost entirely on the Trunks of Large Trees, passing the vast majority of its Existence at a ninety degree angle to what Humans call "upright." The Tree Goat clings to bark and branches with powerful, Hooked Protuberances instead of hooves or hands while grazing on Mosses, Lichens, and Insects. The Tree Goat is considered Beneficial to Trees as it reduces the Habitat of boring insects and other wood pathogens. Living in groups of five to thirty,

Tree Goats often pass their allotted five to seven years circling the trunk of the Tree where they were born, though they can also migrate from tree to tree by passing along Thick Branches, and thus are frequently observed upside down.

The large Spiral Horns of the Tree Goat, a chief identifier, do seem potentially dangerous, and caution is advised in Approach, though no Record of harm to Humans has been Recorded of this Retiring Creature, who seems perfectly content in the deployment of Cautious Retreat over Attack as its primary mode of Self-Preservation.

— Commonly observed. Recorded by A.A.

Mistiness

It is unclear as of this Writing whether Mistiness is an Animal, a Plant, or a Fungus. It consists of airborne Particles too minuscule for detection by the eye. However, congregation of these Atoms precipitate a Purplish Cloud, which floats in Forests at heights between thirty and a hundred feet. A scavenger, Mistiness consumes dead matter ranging from rotten Wood to large Mammals. Although there have been no reports of Living Creatures harmed by Mistiness, it is the view of Tradition and this Writer that passing through the clouds should be avoided.

— Commonly observed. Recorded by A.A.

Candlefly

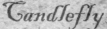

A producer of a potent and Beneficial Bioluminescence, the Candlefly hatches in early spring and, after a brief maiden Flight, appends permanently to the underside of a low-hanging Branch. Over the course of several days its Abdomen extends to a length of five to seven inches, forming a pendent Taper coated in sticky Resin. Once mature, a powerful luminescence ignites at the terminus, which attracts Insects. Mired in the Resin, Nutriment is extracted from these Prisoners by the Candlefly, and they are eventually dissolved and consolidated into the Taper.

By season's end, the Taper has accreted into a Sculpture of shellacked wings, carapaces, and legs, which hardens with the cooling season. The Candlefly lays its eggs within, immediately preceding its own Death.

The Bioluminescent Abdomen continues to illume its surround for several seasons, though the Fly itself is long deceased, its Eggs hatched, and its Young departed. These vacant Candles are frequently brought into Homes for the purpose of beautification and lighting.

— Commonly observed. Recorded by A. A.

Candlefly

Alphabeetle

This Creature is one of the Most Nefarious Pests known.
Were it not for his determined Tolerance toward all
Creatures, this Author would recommend its immediate
and total Eradication.

The Alphabeetle lives in the pages of old Books, eating
the pulp and ink and destroying Knowledge. It is
nearly impossible to spot on casual inspection,
as it has evolved an ingenious method
of Camouflage wherein it resembles one or
another Letter of the Alphabet. The
only Hint of Infestation is found in
the poor Spelling Ability of these
flat-bodied Gluttons. As they do not
know what Letter they Resemble, they
frequently appear as Spelling Errors,
turning, for instance, the work "Book"
into "Bnok." A suspected Alphabeetle can
be Prodded with a Quill to produce its
instinctual Scuttle toward the Book
Spine. Sadly, no Fumigation technique
is known. Infected Books should be
Quarantined and Recopied forthwith.

—Observed and Recorded by A. A.

Squint

The etymology of the term "Squint" is obscure, but it
is thought that "Squint" once meant "Small." This diminu-
tive Forest Mammal lives in colonies of twenty to sixty and is
Extremely Populous, Commonly Sighted, Easily Hunted,
and Edible, advantages that recommend it both to Humans
and to the Forest Lion. Squint meat is rich, strongly grained,
and possesses of a nutty flavor that is Highly Regarded.

— Commonly Observed. Recorded by A. A.
        Recipe by Elazar.

Stuffed Squint

- 1 Squint
- 2 Cups chopped Carrots
- 2 Tablespoon ground Hotroot
- 2 Cups diced Potatoes
- 2 Cups Kale
- 1 large Turnip

Bleed, disembowel, and skin Squint. Thoroughly combine Kale,
Carrots, Potatoes, and ground Hotroot and place inside the Cavity,
blocking the Mouth with the whole Turnip. Skewer Squint (and
turnip) and place over a fire on a Rotisserie to taste. Remove
vegetables from Cavity, carve Squint, and Enjoy. Serves Two

Mesmer Vole

A fascinating example of natural Mesmerism, the small, stub-nosed Mesmer Vole is unique in its ability to Manipulate the activities of other Creatures. The Vole establishes an underground Den early in the Season, around the Entrance to which it spreads a Pheromone smelling of Honey, which attracts a multitude of living Creatures ranging from beetles to elk. Then, using an as-yet-poorly-understood Magnetic Influence, the Vole hypnotizes each visitor to perform its Bidding, accomplishing tasks ranging from maintenance of its Den to Procurement of Comestibles. After enticing sufficient Benefactors, the Vole retreats underground, from which place it manipulates its Entourage.

—Observed and Recorded by Henrift.

Hothead

The Hothead possesses the
highest Body Temperature
of any Creature Known.
It is sometimes called the
Oven Mouse,
and has an
extremely
active Metabolism
resulting in an Average Body Temperature
of 120° F. The Hothead weighs between one and
two pounds and lives in Families of between six and twelve
Individuals, in burrows of Bare Dirt, feeding on Insects
and Roots. Gardeners sometimes regard Hotheads as pests
due to their appetite for Carrots, but these Creatures are
largely Beneficial to Humans, especially in wintertime when
many families install Hothead Burrows under their Homes
to encourage the presence of the Immoderately Toasty
Rodents. A large family of Hotheads can provide considerable
Heat, raising the temperature of a two-room Cottage by up
to Ten Degrees during Cold Months.

— Commonly observed. Recorded by A. A.

Daacht

A small Mammal living in groups of six to ten, the Daacht is most easily identified by its copious coat of cinnamon-colored Fur. During winter Hibernation, its Hair grows so voluminously that the Daacht is completely enveloped, and, if seen, will appear to be a discarded Wig. In springtime when the Daacht awakens, it begins to shed immediately, and large clumps of Hair are deposited on Brambles, which are extremely Beneficial for weaving and wig making.
The Daacht should be approached with caution, as its bite contains a Hormone that sometimes causes Compulsive Behaviors in Humans.

—Observed and Recorded by A.A.

Slow Snake / Slow Snail

Though the name is a misnomer,
it is too widely distributed to
change. The Slow Snake,
however, is not a snake but a snail, and this author is
compelled to encourage the use of the term "Slow Snail."
The misnomer "Snake" arises from early Fatalities associated
with this Deadly Animal, whose bite marks resemble those
left by snakes.

The Slow Snake, more properly Slow Snail, deposits a
pearlescent Track composed of mucous, like most Gastropods.
It feeds upon Blood, which it stores in its Shell. Though
unable to kill a Healthy Person, Children have sometimes
succumbed while Sleeping. Fortunately, because of the Slow
Snake/Snail's diurnal Habit, there is little likelihood of
sustaining a bite while Asleep. Additionally, the Creature
is slow enough to pose no threat in Pursuit. Therefore, only
individuals who make a Habit of sleeping during daylight hours,
such as tired people, are at risk.

The most common Food of the Slow Snake/Snail is bats.
The Creature has been observed crawling to the top of caves and
ingesting the blood of bats, typically killing their Quarry.
Fortunately, once the Shell of the Slow Snail is full with
Blood, it need not feed for an interval of forty to sixty days.

— Commonly observed. Recorded by A. A.

Springer

One of the most startlingly Colorful of Creatures, this large Decoratively plumed Bird is at its most spectacular in spring when its Head sprouts a massive Iridescent Comb containing Feathers up to a foot in length and its Tail, capable of Fanning for Display, is painted in luminous Colors observed nowhere else. These discarded feathers are unsurpassed as Writing Quills.

There is some speculation about the purpose of this Display, which seems such a Poor Camouflage. It appears that the Springer has no natural Predators, though it is neither Dangerous, Poisonous, nor Swift. Thus far, no Human Hunter has killed one either, owing to its Tremendous Beauty. Possibly other animals spare it for the same Reason.

— Commonly observed. Recorded by A.A.

Pulchritude Hound

Named for its singular curatorial impulse, the Pulchritude Hound is one of the few Animals known to express aesthetic Preferences. The Hounds live in packs of thirty to fifty, and during Mating Season each Male becomes enamored of Flowers, and constructs a rude Exhibit by clearing a small patch of Ground. It gathers Flowers, apparently in response to their beauty, and arranges them in accordance with a Logic presently obscure to Human Understanding. Once the males complete their Exhibits, the females tour the cases and select a Mate for the Season based thereon.

—Observed by Henrift. Recorded by A.A.

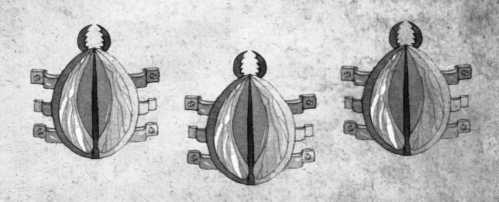

Appleseed Midge

Congregating in annoying Swarms, the appleseed-sized Appleseed Midge spends its short season in the cool shadows of Trees, Buildings, or other Large Structures. The Midges are distressingly Agile and trend toward entanglement in the hair of Passersby, administering a painful Bite and sinking, like a tic, partially below the Skin. Strangely, once a Midge has established itself subcutaneously, others of its kind stay clear. There has never been a record of a single person hosting more than a single Midge in a season. For this reason, and because the Creatures seem to cause no Trouble for the Host, an established Midge is generally left alone until it expires naturally in the autumn and detaches of its own Accord.

— Commonly observed. Recorded by A. A.

The Bestiary

Henrietta had always disliked her house, with its stubby single level and embarrassing peaked roof. The newer houses that surrounded it, two or three levels with nice flat roofs, seemed obviously superior. But now the peaked roof of Henrietta's house was something special—a habitat for a wild housecat, and she was excited to get back to it.

The ride home was quiet. Henrietta's parents both seemed angry, which struck her as odd. Why would finding out that her grandmother had cancer make them mad? They fumed in silence and said nothing to Henrietta by way of explanation.

When the ride finally ended, Henrietta could scarcely contain her desire to get back into the attic. She rushed to the front door of the house and waited impatiently as her father unlocked it. Once inside, she headed immediately in the direction of her room, but her mother stopped her.

"What do you have there?" she asked, pointing at the *Bestiary* that Henrietta held in one hand.

"Al gave it to me," said Henrietta, hoping her mother wouldn't be too interested.

"It's . . . old?" said her mother, holding out one hand. Henrietta reluctantly gave her the book. Her father looked revolted. Her parents both peered at it, trying to untangle the mess of flourishes that composed the title. "What sort of book is it?"

"I don't know yet," said Henrietta.

"Is it age-appropriate?"

"School-district-approved content?"

"Did you just *wink* at me, young lady?" said her mother.

"No!" said Henrietta. *Had* she winked? If so, she was glad she'd finally figured it out.

"I'm worried it will give you a headache," said her father.

"I hadn't thought about that," said her mother, turning the book suspiciously over in her hands.

"It won't," said Henrietta. "I didn't get one when Al showed it to me, and we looked at it for a long time."

Henrietta's mother frowned, but finally returned the book to her. "Put it away if you start to feel ill."

Henrietta moved again toward her room, but again her mother stopped her.

"Before you start your homework, we need to talk about something," she said awkwardly. She began to pick at the pink nail polish on one of her fingers. "Something that happened at the party today." She paused lengthily, formulating a few appropriate euphemisms. Henrietta could see that it would take nearly forever for her to broach the topic. And she just couldn't stand to wait anymore.

"I already know grandma's dying," she said. "Al told me."

Her mother and father both gasped.

"He *what?*" said her mother.

"He said *what?*" said her father.

"He said I didn't need to be protected from it," said Henrietta.

Her father pulled out his cell phone. "I'm calling that man right now," he said.

"You are *grounded*, young lady," said her mother.

"But what did I —" said Henrietta.

"Just go to your room and think about it!" said her mother, too flustered to substantiate her anger. She quickly peeled all of the nail polish off of one finger and started in on the next.

This was exactly what Henrietta had been hoping to hear, and she left immediately as her father began sputtering a voice message to Al.

●•• ••●

Henrietta stopped by the bathroom to grab some sterile gauze before hurrying into her bedroom and closing the door behind. She balanced her chair atop her desk, climbed to the trapdoor, and once again entered the attic, her new book in tow.

The light was much better during the day. The little living room with the couch, coffee table, and wicker chairs looked extremely inviting, and the small table with the dictionary on it reminded Henrietta that she had a word to look up.

Beyond the coffee table and seating, the bookcases towered, covered in an even film of dust. There were several sets, one obscuring the next, largely blocking her view of the rest of the interior, though she could glimpse bits of things back in the shadows: a desk, a sewing table, boxes, a crate, a chest, a dresser, an umbrella stand. The light coming through the windows illuminated more than the moon had the previous night.

She stopped short.

Windows? she thought. How odd . . . she'd never noticed them from outside the house before. She shook her head. A mystery to solve later.

The wild house cat had moved away from the trapdoor, and reclined now on the couch. It looked better. It held up its head easily. Its gray-furred ears twitched this way and that, homing in on the small sounds of the attic, and its enormous green eyes with their wide black pupils watched her.

Henrietta placed the *Bestiary* on the coffee table, and approached the cat. It stood warily on its long, thin legs. This was the first time she'd seen it at its full height, and it was considerably taller than an ordinary housecat.

"I want to change your bandages," said Henrietta, "to prevent infection."

The cat sat, and Henrietta gently removed the tape and gauze she'd applied the night before. The wound looked bad, but better. It was scabbing and didn't appear swollen or infected. She replaced the bloodied gauze with a fresh square.

"I think it's okay," she said. She reached out to pet the cat, hoping to comfort it, but the moment she moved her hand toward it, it retreated to the far end of the couch. "I wish you'd let me pet you," she said. She thought she would never get enough of looking at it. It was the strangest, most wonderful creature she'd ever seen. "I wonder if you're hungry." Her eyes wandered over to the coffee table, and the *Bestiary*. She studied the baroque lettering on the cover, and then

took out her phone to look up the word. But the phone was frozen again, just like the other night. She tapped the screen, and then returned it to her pocket as she remembered the dictionary on the table between the wicker chairs. She brought it to the couch and flipped through the Bs.

> Bestiary (n) *bes'che-er'e* A compendium of animals, commonly including those fictitious and those extinct.

She looked up *compendium* ("a concise collection of detailed information"), and then opened the *Bestiary*. The pages were thick, rough, and discolored into a variety of yellows, unlike the smooth plastic pages she was familiar with.

The book's text was written in a loopy, long cursive. Henrietta marveled at how much time must have gone into the making of it. Early in the year, Ms. Span had shown the class the cursive alphabet, though they hadn't ever practiced it. This book was written more beautifully than the precise, typed examples their class had seen. It flowed like a river. Henrietta touched it with her fingers and followed the lines of the word *Bestiary* on the title page. Below was another line, which she had to look at for some time before she could unravel its meaning. "Researched and Written by Aristotle Alcott, Henrift, and Many Friends."

She wondered if this Henrift might be Henrift Andi, Humanitarian and Forward Thinker. The movie at school never mentioned him being an author.

Henrietta turned a few more of the brittle pages. Some of the paper crumbled under her fingers. She reached the table of contents and scanned it until she found a section labeled "House Animals," and the subsection "Housecats—Wild."

It seemed unbelievable that this book should have such an entry. She'd never read or heard about wild housecats anywhere before today. Why didn't her teachers ever mention them? She wondered, for the first time, who decided what would be taught at school. Henrietta noted the page number of the chapter on House Animals, and flipped to it.

Endemic to Attics and Root Cellars. Because of its habitual reclusiveness and a lack of Research (due partly to difficulty of retaining Specimens and partly to poor persistence in captivity), few facts about the animal are known with Certainty.

The Wild Housecat's diet remains unobserved; despite its probable unreliability, it seems appropriate to report the opinion of Tradition, as a popular Children's Rhyme suggests a subsistence on "Cobwebs and Rat Tails, Dust and Rust."

This Animal is considered beneficial to Humankind, as it is held not only to control Rat populations, but also to keep houses free of Spider Webs and Insects. For this reason, many Homes contain so-called "Cat Halls," thought to encourage Ingress and Egress.

Wild Housecats are thought to possess considerable intelligence, and Tradition holds that, in some respects, they may be the equal of Humans. Such Holdings, also, have sadly not been subjected to verification through the Scientific Method.

—A.A.

After reading the entry, Henrietta went back over it with the dictionary, looking up the unfamiliar words. She turned to the cat.

"They don't know what you eat," she said. "Maybe cobwebs."

She went to a bookcase, plucked a web from the corner of a shelf, and smeared it onto the sofa cushion near the cat. The cat flicked out one paw and patted the web. Then it yawned widely, and Henrietta saw its long, white teeth. It curled up on the couch, and evinced no further interest in its proposed dinner.

"I'd better go back before my parents miss me," said Henrietta. "I hope you keep getting better."

Intentional Detention

Henrietta always looked forward to Saturdays, her only day off from school, but every time one arrived, it soon became yesterday. Now, early on Sunday morning, idly watching plumes of exhaust erupt from tailpipes onto the blacktop, the next weekend seemed impossibly distant. Today was a little different from an average Sunday, though. For once something had *really happened* the day before, and furthermore she had friends to tell about it.

Gary approached from up the block. He was a large boy, and a clumsy walker whose feet frequently tangled with one another or their surroundings. Today, he arrived just as the bus opened its door. Cars honked, annoyed at the holdup even though it happened at precisely the same time every day.

"GET IN SHAPE WITH
LURMY'S NEGATIVE-CALORIE ENCHILADA!"

"TINCAN TELECOMM'S SKIPPING-STONE PHONE IS
PERFECT FOR ATHLETES!"

The children boarded and buckled in. As the bus rolled forward and the sounding horns diminished, Henrietta twisted toward Gary in her network of straps. "I have something to tell you."

"What?" said Gary. He looked interested, but his thick eyebrows loomed tiredly. It seemed to require great effort from him to prop them up in the mornings.

"Um . . . well, you should *see* it."

Gary grinned sleepily. "You have to tell me you have to show me something?"

"It's at my house. But I can't show you till Wednesday." Henrietta sighed. "I got grounded for finding out something."

"What was it?" said Gary.

"My grandma's dying," said Henrietta. "But my parents wanted it a secret."

"I'm sorry." Gary looked thoughtful. "When my dad died, my mom didn't want me to know either. She told me he was on a cruise."

"That's terrible," said Henrietta. She could scarcely imagine such a brazen lie.

"Yeah," said Gary. "They were divorced, so I didn't see him much anyway." He paused. It seemed obvious from his expression that it had been a terrible secret to discover. "Are you sad about your grandma?"

"Kind of," she said. "I want to be. But I don't see her very much."

"My dad used to send me a card every year for my birthday," said Gary. "That's how I knew he wasn't really on a cruise—because no card came."

Henrietta's grandmother also sent Henrietta a card each year on her birthday, and this struck her suddenly as very sad—not that the cards would stop coming, but that they'd been her grandmother's most consistent presence.

Gary brightened a little bit. "Hey, you know what? I bet I *could* come over today if you want."

"How?" said Henrietta.

"I just thought of a plan. First, we'll both have to get detention."

"Why?"

"You'll have to see," he said, smiling. His eyes looked more awake as he contemplated his mischief.

●•·•●

This particular Sunday was the first of the month, which meant Physical Safety Period, led by a chubby, pale, balding man named Mr. Safety, who taught his one subject throughout the district, moving from school to school. He never remembered the students' names, and Ms. Span was always present to make sure everyone behaved. It was in Mr. Safety's class that Henrietta had first seen *Watch Out for Pirates*, one of the most exciting movies ever.

Ms. Span's class walked together in a line down the hall to the Physical Safety room, a small gymnasium with a cushioned floor. As they entered, Mr. Safety blew a whistle that hung from a lanyard around his neck.

"LINES OF FIVE!" he barked. The class formed lines of five students each.

"WE'RE GOING TO DO A JUMPING JACK!" said Mr. Safety. "FEET TOGETHER, ARMS LOOSE. WHEN I WHISTLE, JUMP AND BRING YOUR FEET SHOULDER-WIDTH APART, ARMS OVERHEAD, EXCEPT FOR . . ." Here, he consulted a list on his phone of the names of students whose parents didn't want them to do a jumping jack. "CLARENCE, HIROKI, JOSÉ, AND GARY!"

He whistled. The remainder of the students jumped, put their feet shoulder-width apart, and held their arms overhead.

"COOL DOWN!" said Mr. Safety. "Walk in place." He paced along the lines. "Sit!" he barked. The class sat. "WE'RE GOING TO DO A SIT-UP. LIE ON YOUR BACKS, EXCEPT... AMBER, GABRIELLE, AND GARY. EVERYONE ELSE, WHEN I SAY SO, SIT UP. BUT NOT TOO FAST OR YOU'LL GET HERNIAS. YOU DO NOT WANT HERNIAS."

Henrietta sensed Gary in the row next to her, gesturing covertly. "What?" she whispered.

"Look!" Gary pointed to the end of the last row of students. There were five kids there, with Clarence Frederick at the very back. But there was someone else—behind Clarence. Someone who was clearly not a kid.

"Who is it?" Gary said.

Henrietta stared. She blinked and stared again. What she saw there was not a person, though it kind of looked like one. It was the size of an adult, but its face was not a normal adult face. Its skin was pale yellow and even, like pudding smoothed over a tiny nose and an even tinier chin—its small mouth dangled precariously just above. It was dressed in yellow pants and a yellow button-up shirt, and it lay on its back just like the students, its hands by its sides. Its fingers were bizarre, long translucent tapers, like candles. For a moment, it flickered out like a switched-off fluorescent light. When it reappeared, it had changed position: its pale yellow eyes were staring right at Henrietta and Gary.

"SIT UP!" said Mr. Safety. The class did its careful sit-up, and the creature participated obediently.

"STAND!" said Mr. Safety.

The class, and the creature, stood.

"ALL RIGHT EVERYONE. THIS TIME, *TEN* JUMPING JACKS, EXCEPT . . . GARY, JOSÉ, AND BELINDA. WHEN I WHISTLE, YOU COUNT. READY?"

"Ready, Mr. Safety!" said the class.

Weeeh! went Mr. Safety's whistle, and everyone jumped, including the creature.

"ONE!" said the class. "TWO!"

The creature stopped at Two. It stepped away from its line, and strode purposefully toward Henrietta and Gary. Along the way, as it passed other students, it reached out with its long, waxy index finger and tapped them on their foreheads. No one seemed to notice, or see the creature at all.

"Wh-what is it?" Henrietta stuttered.

"It's coming over here!" said Gary, backing out of his line.

"THREE! FOUR!" said the class.

Then another voice sounded, above everything. It was Ms. Span, and her tone was sharp. "Gary and Henrietta!" she said. "Quit clowning!"

"FIVE! SIX!" said the class.

"Run!" said Henrietta as the creature closed on them.

"I'm . . . not supposed to run," said Gary, his voice shaking.

"*Go!*" said Henrietta, and she shoved Gary in front of her. They fled.

"Stop!" Ms. Span yelled as they departed their line and zipped through the one adjacent, interrupting the jumping jacks of several students.

"SEVEN!" said the class.

"Oh my!" said Mr. Safety as Henrietta and Gary skidded from line to line, causing considerable confusion.

"EIGHT!" yelled some students. "SIX!" yelled others. The lines began to break up as Henrietta and Gary desperately pushed through, weaving toward the front of the room, toward Mr. Safety.

"Take care now!" said Mr. Safety nervously, holding up one hand as if to ward off their approach. He placed his whistle in his mouth, preparing to blow.

"It's gaining!" yelled Gary, glancing back. The creature wasn't running, exactly—it flickered after them, disappearing and reappearing in a series of approaching snapshots.

Gary's backward glance was poorly timed. He did not see Clarice Sodje looming up before him, right in the middle of her eighth, or maybe ninth, jumping jack. Gary and Clarice were two of the larger kids in the class, and their impact was considerable. Clarice was mid-jump when they collided, and she and Gary crashed to the padded floor in a grand sprawl. Henrietta was right behind, and there was no time for her to stop. She tripped over them both and went flying right into the soft, unprepared stomach of Mr. Safety.

Weeeeeeeeeeeh! shrilled the whistle as she and Mr. Safety tumbled backwards. Mister Safety landed squarely on his back and expelled the remainder of his breath in a rush that popped the whistle from his mouth. It shot to the limit of its lanyard and snapped back, smacking him in the eye. "Weeeeeeeeeeeh!" went the sound again—but it wasn't the whistle this time. It was Mr. Safety himself, and this final falsetto cry was followed by a series of agonized gasps as he struggled for the breath that had been knocked out of him.

Henrietta landed to the side and scrambled forward, looking back to check on Gary, who had now untangled himself from Clarice and was gaining his feet.

"TEN!" said the few members of class who'd managed to keep count during the fracas.

"Gary! Wait!" said Henrietta. Her glance back had revealed that the creature was no longer pursuing them. It was gone—vanished.

Gary turned around, searching. "It must be somewhere," he said, eyes darting this way and that. "Oh, wow, it was . . . that was . . . *the thing*! The one I saw when you got your headache!"

There was no opportunity for further discussion. Ms. Span, who had just called the nurse's office to order some medical assistance for Mr. Safety (who lay splayed and gasping on the ground, both hands covering his injured eye), returned her phone to her pocket and grabbed both Henrietta and Gary by the ears.

"We are returning to our classroom, *now*!" she barked at the class. "Line up and follow!" She dragged Henrietta and Gary with her into the hallway, the class obediently following, tittering animatedly at how exciting it had all been, and what ridiculous weirdos Henrietta and Gary were.

Gary's plan was now, for better or worse, in motion: they'd earned the detention they'd wanted.

●·· ·●

At the close of the school day, as the rest of the students filed out to the buses after completing their final typing practice on the subject of autumn ("I WILL NOT JUMP IN A PILE OF LEAVES"), Henrietta and Gary stayed in their seats. Gary winked conspiratorially at Henrietta, who tried to wink back and surprised herself by succeeding.

"Henrietta and Gary, you will spend your detention today sitting quietly and regretting your behavior," said Ms. Span from the front. "Did you know that our class ranked in the thirtieth systemwide percentile today in no small part because of your disobedience?"

"We're sorry," they said in unison.

"Say it to yourselves, not to me," said Ms. Span.

Time crawled by. Ms. Span worked at her computer up front, putting together her materials for the following day. Once the buses had left, Gary gave Henrietta a significant look. Then he turned to the front of the room and said, loudly, "Mom?"

Henrietta's eyes widened. Ms. Span looked up, but didn't remove her glasses—obviously surprised. She squinted at Gary, and then at Henrietta, and then at Gary again.

"Yes, Gary?" she said evenly.

"Can we give Henrietta a ride home? Because she missed her bus, and, you know, we live right across the street from her."

Ms. Span removed her glasses. "Absolutely not," she said. "I don't know her parents at all. I don't want there to be any misunderstandings."

Henrietta was dumbstruck, observing for the first time that Gary and Ms. Span had the exact same thick, black eyebrows that met in the middle.

"We could call her parents and ask," said Gary.

This, then, was it: Gary's plan. Henrietta saw that for it to succeed, she'd have to help.

"My mom would appreciate it," she said. "She's probably working on dinner

88

right now. I can give you my number." Henrietta reached into her pocket for her phone.

"It's already in the school network," said Ms. Span. Without another word, she dialed Henrietta's house. "Hello. Is this Mrs. Gad-Fly?" she said. "Yes, that's right. Henrietta's teacher. My son and your daughter are both here for detention today due to some regretful misbehavior," here she paused to glare out across the room at the two of them, "and they've missed their bus. Would it be convenient for you if I gave Henrietta a ride home? Gary has just pointed out that we live across the street from you." There was a long pause. "Twenty minutes. It will be nice to meet you, too." Ms. Span pocketed the phone and stood from her terminal. "We'd best get going."

"Great!" said Gary. He looked at Henrietta and waggled his eyebrows. The two of them stepped into the hall while Ms. Span gathered her things.

"She's your *mom*?" Henrietta whispered.

"Yeah," said Gary. "No one knows, so don't tell." Their whispered voices echoed in the empty hallway, bouncing off the giant mural image of happy children below the words "Sensible, Efficient, Education (S.E.E!)"

"I won't," said Henrietta. She shook her head. "It's so weird."

"To you, maybe," said Gary.

Ms. Span emerged from the room and the three of them proceeded down the hall, following a yellow line on the floor through a set of doors and down a flight of stairs to the parking garage. "Henrietta, it will be interesting to meet your parents," said Ms. Span. "I didn't know Gary had told you I was his mother. You two must be good friends."

"We are," said Henrietta.

"Because we sit together," said Gary. "I've been helping Henrietta bring up her scores. We're best friends now."

As they approached Ms. Span's car, a blue station wagon, a recorded voice issued from a speaker on the cement floor of the garage.

"THE SCHOOL DISTRICT IS NOT RESPONSIBLE FOR ANY INJURY RECEIVED WHILE ENTERING, LEAVING, OR TRAVELING THROUGH THE PREMISES."

"Can Henrietta and I sit in the back?" said Gary, as Ms. Span unlocked the doors.

"Buckle all of your seat belts," said Ms. Span. They fastened themselves into the rear seats. The engine started and the car's computer came online.

"WHERE ARE YOU GOING?" it asked.

"Home for Henrietta Gad-Fly," said Ms. Span.

"FOLLOW THE SIGNS TO THE LOT EXIT AND TURN LEFT." Ms. Span navigated accordingly. "WHILE YOU DRIVE, WOULD YOU LIKE TO HEAR SOME ADVERTISEMENTS FOR PRODUCTS THAT MAY INTEREST YOU?"

"No," said Ms. Span.

"THANK YOU," said the car. "THIS THANK-YOU WAS BROUGHT TO YOU BY MIRACLE MEDICAL'S EARHELPER. EARHELPER IS AN AUDIO REFINEMENT DEVICE THAT REDUCES TRAFFIC NOISE WHILE INCREASING VOICE CLARITY. EVER HAVE TROUBLE HEARING WHAT YOUR CAR IS SAYING WHILE YOU DRIVE? WITH EARHELPER, YOU'LL NEVER SAY 'WHAT?' AGAIN."

Ms. Span reached the parking lot exit and passed through the pay station.

"SEVENTY DOLLARS AND SIXTY-SEVEN CENTS HAS BEEN AUTOMATICALLY WITHDRAWN FROM YOUR ACCOUNT," said the car. "THANK YOU FOR USING AUTODEDUCT. YOUR CONVENIENCE IS OUR

REWARD. TURN LEFT."

"So, Henrietta," said Ms. Span. "Which house do you live in?"

"The one with the peaked roof."

"*Oh*," said Ms. Span. She was silent for a few moments. "Is that . . . very old?"

"It's safe," said Henrietta.

"But, your headaches," said Mrs. Span. "You're getting House Sick, aren't you?"

"Nobody really knows for sure," said Henrietta.

"Gary," said Ms. Span, "I think you should wait in the car when we arrive. I'm worried your House Sickness might come back if you go in."

"Oh, Mom," said Gary, "I haven't had a headache in a long time. Can't I come in just for a minute? *Ple-ease?*" His *please* utilized a special tone that children have, which can crack almost any parental decree, and Ms. Span reluctantly assented.

They drove in silence for a while, Gary occasionally waggling his eyebrows at Henrietta to call attention to the perfect success of his plan.

When the car reached their block, Ms. Span turned left into Henrietta's driveway, and the engine stopped automatically. Henrietta and Gary extricated themselves from their seat belts and stepped onto the driveway with Ms. Span.

"I can't wait to show—" Henrietta began, but she stopped halfway through the sentence.

"What?" said Gary.

Henrietta pointed toward her roof. There were two dim squares near the top of the house where the siding was a slightly darker color.

"What are you looking at, Henrietta?" said Ms. Span.

Henrietta retracted her hand. "It's a different color," she said. But what she was thinking was, *Where are the attic windows?*

They reached the front door, and Henrietta's mother opened it, wearing a bright yellow blouse and brown polyester slacks.

"Hi, Mom," said Henrietta.

"Hi, honey," she said, looking not at Henrietta, but at Ms. Span. "Hello, Ms. Span," she said, holding out her hand. "I'm Aline, Henrietta's mother."

"It's nice to meet you, Aline. Call me Margaret."

"Please, come in," said Henrietta's mother. Henrietta and Gary entered, and Ms. Span cautiously followed. They stepped into the sitting room, a space Henrietta and her parents didn't use much, though it contained some of their nicest furniture: a shiny vinyl couch, two chairs with faux-leather backs, and a long plastic table with legs shaped like columns of cell phones, which Henrietta's mother had bought for her father when he got his job at TinCan TeleComm. The table was empty but for a single glass vase that contained a fabric rose tastefully adorned with plastic dewdrops.

Ms. Span studied the room, especially the ceiling. "I don't think I've ever been in a house this old," she said.

"Sorry," said Henrietta's mother. "We're moving out soon."

"Not until the end of the school year, though, right?" said Henrietta. Her mother had said this to visitors before, so Henrietta wasn't too alarmed by it, but she still felt the need to speak up.

Her mother smiled a little awkwardly. "No, of course not," she said. In fact, it was unlikely that they would move at all unless they could find someone to buy the place for more than it was worth.

"Gary and I used to live in a place almost this old," said Ms. Span. "The city finally bought it from us and demolished it."

"That sounds wonderful," said Henrietta's mother.

"Mom, can I show Gary my room?" said Henrietta.

"Of course, but Gary should ask his mother."

"Can I, Mom?" said Gary.

"I worry you'll get House Sick," said Ms. Span.

"Does Gary get House Sick?" said Henrietta's mother.

"He used to," said Ms. Span, "until we moved."

"*Ple-ease?*" said both children at once.

Scaredy Gary

"Whdat was that thing?" said Gary, as soon as Henrietta shut the door. She shivered, recalling the ghastly, flicking creature.

"I don't know," she said.

"And why *us*?" said Gary.

Henrietta shook her head. She took out her cell phone, thinking to look it up. "Search: Ugly yellow creature," she said into it.

"THANK YOU FOR SEARCHING WITH TINCAN TELECOMM," said a friendly, computerized woman's voice. "YOUR SEARCH FOR UGLY YELLOW CREATURE MAKES ME WONDER IF YOU WOULD LIKE TO BUY SOME YELLOW RAIN BOOTS. WOULD YOU LIKE TO BUY SOME YELLOW RAIN BOOTS?"

Henrietta hung up. She looked at Gary. "I don't know how much time we have before you have to go," she said, "and there's something I have to show you, no matter what." She went to her desk and pulled out her plastic chair. Her computer's counting program was running: 36,548. Henrietta looked twice at it. That was odd—that's where it was the last time she'd looked.

"It was so strange-looking," Gary mused, still thinking about the creature. "Not like a real person at all. And its fingers, tapping everyone!" Gary held his hands out, letting his fingers droop forward limply, and then wiggled his pointer fingers. "Hey, what are you doing?" he said.

Henrietta had placed the chair on top of her desk. "You have to promise not to tell anyone about this," she said.

"I promise," said Gary.

Without further pause, Henrietta climbed onto her desk, and then onto the chair. She put her hand against the ceiling and pushed.

The trapdoor opened.

Gary gasped.

"Shh!" said Henrietta, glaring down at him. "Follow me, but be quiet."

"Follow you?" he said. "But I *can't*." The pitch of his voice rose as he spoke, like air squeaking from a balloon.

Henrietta was a little surprised. On the bus the other day, Gary had seemed fearless. But she'd also noticed he was the only student to be released from every exercise during Physical Safety. "Why not?" she said.

"I . . . could fall."

"We'll be careful," said Henrietta. "This kind of thing is the reason people invented carefulness in the first place." Without allowing him another moment to protest, she grabbed the edge of the trapdoor and pulled herself into the attic.

Gary followed, reluctantly. He wrestled his squat body onto the chair, and then dragged himself up with great effort. As he emerged into the shadowy space, Henrietta whispered, "Welcome to the attic!"

Gary sat up and looked around in amazement, his eyes lighting on the bookcases, the coffee table, the windows, and finally on the wild housecat. He emitted a mousey squeak when he saw it, and held up his hands. The cat stood from its seat on the couch.

"This is a wild housecat," said Henrietta. "It isn't particularly dangerous." She paused. "Gary. Open your eyes." Gary opened them a tiny bit. To the housecat, Henrietta said, "This is my friend Gary. He's not particularly dangerous, either." The cat watched Gary with its huge green eyes.

Gary stepped forward from the trapdoor. "*Wild* housecat?" he said.

"I found it up here," said Henrietta. "It's hurt, but it's getting better."

"What happened to it?"

"It got stabbed," said Henrietta, "but I don't know how."

Gary continued looking around, his eyes probing back toward the obscure, shadowy interior behind the bookcases. "This place is huge," he said.

"And you know what's really weird?" said Henrietta. "No one knows we're up here."

Gary froze. His black eyebrows bunched together. He opened his mouth and stuck his tongue out, and squinted, and balled his hands up into fists. "Auuughoo . . ." he moaned. The next thing Henrietta knew, he had launched himself to the trapdoor and scrambled down to the chair. In his rush, however, he misstepped, lunged sideways, and fell onto the desk and then to the floor with a powerful thud.

Henrietta hurried after to find him sitting next to her bed, staring intently into her BedCam. Henrietta listened carefully to see if her mother or Ms. Span had heard the commotion. Miraculously, they hadn't.

"I got scared," said Gary, his eyes glued to the BedCam.

"You sure did," said Henrietta. "That's broken by the way." She pointed to the BedCam. "It can't see you."

Gary turned to her. "Really, *really* scary up there."

"Scaredy Gary," said Henrietta.

Gary frowned. "What?"

"It's what the kids were saying on the bus."

"Well, it isn't true," Gary snapped.

"Then let's go back up," said Henrietta.

Gary set his features determinedly. "Right. Yes. Okay. No problem."

Again, he followed Henrietta through the inky opening, being careful not to stumble off the chair. Henrietta closed the door after them and watched Gary as he turned around in the space, taking everything in.

"Nobody knows," he said to himself. He clenched his fists. Henrietta thought he was going to panic a second time, but he seemed to fight it off. He relaxed. "I'm all right," he said. He strode purposefully over to the windows and looked out through them.

"Remember when we were outside, when I pointed?" said Henrietta. "You can't see the windows outside—they're covered."

"Wow!" said Gary, pointing through them.

"Shh!" Henrietta was still worried the adults would overhear.

"*Look!*" Gary whispered intently. Henrietta joined him and gazed out, down at the neighborhood outside.

The neighborhood she saw wasn't hers.

The Wikkeling

Henrietta and Gary's new friend Rose was very smart, but most people—even her parents, who loved her—thought she was a bit dull. She'd often stare vacantly out into space, and she seemed unresponsive at times or said things that didn't make sense. But there was a reason for this. Rose could see something that other people couldn't see—a creature called the Wikkeling.

She had first encountered it when she was very young, before she'd started school. She'd been out for a walk with her father along an old alleyway behind a hospital, to her father's favorite dumpster. The dumpster was made of clean, white plastic, and it was full of unused hospital supplies such as medical tape, unopened boxes of bandages, and even surgical tools—items her father used for repairing books, which was his hobby.

He had opened the top of the dumpster and disappeared inside while Rose kept a lookout (because people don't generally like it when you steal their trash). Once she was alone, however, she felt a strange sensation, like someone was standing next to her. She turned.

Its fine, thin hair was yellow, and its face smooth and young, with a strange small nose and chin. It wore yellow pants and a yellow button-up shirt, and its body flickered like a fluorescent light.

"Who are you?" Rose said, startled.

"I'M WIKKELING," it said. Its lips didn't form the words when it spoke—it opened its round mouth and the sound spilled out, scratchy like an old recording.

It raised one hand revealing five extremely long, waxy fingers, and before Rose could react, it tapped her on the forehead with one of them, and flicked out of sight, disappearing in an instant. Rose immediately felt nauseous. Her head throbbed. She began to cry, and her father heard her and climbed immediately out of the dumpster. As he reached her, she lost consciousness.

She awakened later in her bedroom, her parents kneeling next to her, concern clouding their features. She tried to explain what had happened, but it didn't make much sense, even to her.

After that, Rose saw the Wikkeling often. If she was in the park, it stood near the swing set. If she was in class, it walked past the coatrack. It spent most of its time tapping people on the forehead, just like it had tapped her. But other people didn't seem to mind. They didn't get headaches.

Rose was extremely frightened of the Wikkeling, and quickly learned that for some reason it rarely went into her house, so she spent as much time as she could inside, deep in the interior of the old place, which was filled with old books.

●· · ·●

Rose lived far out on the sparkling plain of the Addition, where the homes were constructed entirely of plastic and featured amenities such as disposable bathtubs, antibiotic tabletops, digital windows, and underground parking. But the house Rose lived in with her parents was quite unlike these. Rose's house was very, very old. It was unique in the Addition—an ancient island in a sea of newness.

Rose's parents referred to their house as the Library. The walls all through the place were lined with shelves packed tight with books of all sizes and topics. The house was enormous. The main level and all of the three upper floors were full of reading material. Some of the rooms had hand-painted signs over the doorways describing different genres, such as COOKERY or COMPUTERS. The house had been this way since Rose could remember, and she and her parents were rarely alone there.

Visitors often happened by to borrow or return books, and Rose knew them all by name. Her parents called them the Subscribers. They didn't look like the other people in this story, with new clothes, tidy haircuts, and the latest personal accoutrements. The Subscribers showed up in thick layers of old clothes, often spotted with grease or fringed with dirt. Their shoes looked as though they'd been repaired many times. They carried backpacks, into which they stowed the books they borrowed, and from which they produced the books they returned.

The Subscribers never entered the house through the front door. They arrived from the back, via a narrow alleyway directly abutting the plastic, windowless wall of a skyscraper behind. They were admitted only after supplying a complex secret knock that involved both knocks and scratches, and after Rose or her parents looked through the peephole at them. Once they were recognized and admitted into the kitchen, they'd be offered a cookie.

"Don't let anyone in if you don't know them, or if they don't know the knock," Rose's mother told her once. The Subscribers had all signed a contract after being interviewed by Rose's parents. The Library Use Agreement ran as follows:

> *I promise, as a Subscriber to the Library, to:*
>> *Return what I borrow*
>> *Donate new materials when possible*
>> *Conserve the Collection*
>> *Be a good friend to Rose*

Conserve the Collection meant *Repair the Books*. Once per week the Subscribers gathered to do book maintenance. Rose's father, who had been trained once upon a time as a doctor, was the lead conservator, and as such many of the repaired books somewhat resembled repaired people. Rose's father would often do his work as if in an operating theater, with Rose assisting.

"Thread," he would say, and Rose would hand him thread.

"Glue," he would say, and Rose would hand him the glue.

Because of all of this, Rose knew how to fix books before she knew how to read them. She'd reattached bindings, installed new endpapers, and even affixed new covers to books that arrived stripped, sometimes making her own artwork after her parents told her what the book was about.

Rose's life in the Library was also a surprisingly athletic one. The Library was so large that living in it required a healthy amount of walking, especially going up and down stairs, because the four-level place had neither escalators nor elevators. Two levels, the main level and the second level, had thirty-foot high ceilings with bookcases stretching from top to bottom. These walls had wheeled ladders built into them, which could be rolled from place to place.

Rose's parents encouraged her to use the ladders, and she quickly displayed a natural talent for climbing that was a bit mystifying given how slight she appeared. She could climb before she could walk, and became consequently good at falling without getting hurt.

"She'll swing from her ponytail when she grows up," her mother once predicted as she watched Rose leap from ladder to ladder.

"We'll see whose hair she has when she grows up," said her father, laughing. While her mother's hair was long, blonde, and straight, her father's hair was black and curly. Rose's, so far, was in between.

●•• •●

That was the life of the house's back door: the life of the Library. The house also had a front door, which was seldom used. Visitors at the front door were nicely dressed, and they came from cars they parked in the slim driveway. They were treated very cautiously by Rose's parents, and were never invited in. This was one of the first categories Rose ever understood. *There are two kinds of people: those who come through the kitchen with the secret knock, and those who come to the front.*

A few weeks before Rose had started kindergarten, she'd watched her mother answer the front door and talk with a woman whose hair stood in perfect, rigid blond ringlets. The woman wanted to discuss the parent-teacher association at Rose's school. When the woman left, Rose asked, "Do the front door people ever meet the kitchen door people?"

Her mother put her hands on Rose's shoulders. "Rosie," she said, "they don't. And it's very important that they never do. When you start school in the fall, all the kids you'll meet will be front door people. I need you to not ever tell anyone about the Subscribers—not friends, or teachers, or anyone. Do you understand?"

"It's not alright for us to have all of these books?" said Rose.

"The books are fine," said her mother. "The problem is us. You, your father, and I live here secretly. No one, except for the Subscribers, knows we're here. This house is supposed to be empty. If you tell anyone that we're living here, we'll have to leave forever."

"But people come and talk to you at the front door all the time," said Rose.

"We're tricking them for now," said her mother. "We said we own the place. Hopefully, they won't look into it any further."

This issue proved so important that her parents came to her bedside that night and repeated the whole conversation. Then, at breakfast the next morning, they talked it over a third time.

●·· ··●

At the moment, Rose sat at the small kitchen table on the ground floor of the Library, eating a bowl of corn cereal. The kitchen door opened behind her, and a waft of lilac scented air entered from the alleyway as her mother stepped into the house and closed the door behind. She took a chair opposite Rose, and set her bags on the floor: a cloth sack filled with groceries and a backpack constructed of stitched-together inner tubes from old bicycle tires.

"Hello, Rosie," she said. She kissed Rose on the forehead. "Is your father home?"

"He's in Political Science," said Rose around a mouthful of cereal. Political Science was a small section in the northwest corner of the fourth floor, a cozy wood-lined room with a stained-glass window depicting a boy and girl walking along a dirt road, carrying schoolbooks in their hands.

Her mother's cell phone rang, a chirping sound like a cricket. She dug it from her pocket and saw GAD-FLY on the screen. "Hello?" she said. "Oh, yes— of course I remember you." She paused. "No, Rose doesn't have her own phone. But she's here, if you'd like to talk to her." She held out the phone to Rose. "It's for you."

Through the Windows

enrietta and Gary gazed down in wonder at a street they'd never seen before—a broad, one-lane brick boulevard planted on both sides with enormous, leafy maples whose branches stretched out to touch Henrietta's house.

People strolled up and down paths on either side—a couple arm in arm, a man walking a dog, a group of grandparents with grandchildren. Everyone's clothes were of a strange style that Henrietta thought she'd seen once or twice in old pictures. Men and women alike were dressed in wool coats, buttoned across the front over wide lapels, and sported hats of a variety of styles, some with brightly colored feathers protruding jauntily from hat bands. Everyone, from little boys to old women, wore brown or black dress shoes.

Gary was the first to master his surprise sufficiently to say something. "The houses look like yours." Across the street they could see a row of homes with pitched, shingled roofs. The general style was the same for all, but each house was different from its neighbors. It was as if ten people had each been asked to draw a circle three inches across, and the ten circles that resulted were similar, but also different depending on who made each. A few of the houses were one story, like Henrietta's, but some were two. Several had open front porches, one with a porch swing, and some had no porch at all. From the chimney of one house billowed dark smoke, illuminated occasionally by tiny embers. Inside the front room of another, Henrietta saw several candles burning.

"Our house is old," said Henrietta. "It was my grandmother's. All of *those* houses . . ." she trailed off.

"They became like mine," said Gary.

They were both thinking the same thought, but neither spoke it right away because it sounded ridiculous.

"This is the *past*," Henrietta whispered finally. "It sort of makes sense, I mean, why the windows are blocked off when we're outside, but not here. If we're looking into the past—the windows weren't blocked yet."

Golden-green light filtered through the tops of the trees. Below, the brick street turned the sunlight that reached it into cinnamon. As the two continued to stare, their eyes fell upon an object in the middle of the boulevard in front of Henrietta's house. It resembled an enormous, irregularly shaped table.

"That's the biggest picnic bench I've ever seen," said Gary.

"*Is* it a picnic bench?" said Henrietta. A couple of passersby stopped and sat on its edge, conversing. "I think it's . . . a stump!"

"You mean, from a tree?" said Gary. "Like in the history unit at school?" Henrietta knew what Gary was referring to—a movie called *They Built with Trees*, about how people used to make things out of wood. "It can't be a stump," Gary mused. "Stumps aren't that big. You could park four cars on that!"

"But it is," said Henrietta.

"Wow," said Gary, and he looked up, obviously trying to imagine the enormity of the tree that once grew there. "Hey," he said. "What do you suppose will happen if we go outside now? Will it be now, or then?"

They opened the trapdoor. Henrietta looked at the housecat, who silently watched from the couch. Before it on the coffee table sat the open *Bestiary*.

"It looks like the cat's been reading," Henrietta joked.

Gary laughed. "Studying for the Competency Exam!"

They dropped into Henrietta's room and returned to the living room, where their mothers were still talking, sitting on the couch.

"Ready to go already?" said Ms. Span as Gary entered.

"Um . . . actually, if it's okay, Henrietta and I are going to work on homework together. I thought I'd help her with math."

"That would be wonderful, Gary," said Henrietta's mother. "I'm sure Henrietta would appreciate it."

"I will," said Henrietta. "And we were just going to also . . . "

"Go outside for a second!" said Gary.

The two children, nodding in unison, rushed to the front door and exited onto the sidewalk.

Before them stretched the same scene they saw every day: a four-lane asphalt road crammed with cars. Traffic lights winked. Enormous plastic houses squatted behind green squares of fake turf.

"I wonder when they widened the street," said Gary.

"I guess things had to get bigger," said Henrietta. "Did the clothes those people wore remind you of anyone?"

"Through the windows?" said Gary. He shook his head.

"Rose—with the headache. She wears a wool shirt sometimes."

"You're right," said Gary.

"We should call her," said Henrietta, stepping back inside. "We could invite her over."

They entered the living room to find Gary's mother preparing to leave.

"Gary, I'm glad you're going to help Henrietta. But be on time for dinner, and be *careful* when you cross the street."

"I will, Mom," said Gary.

Ms. Span turned to Henrietta's mother. "It was a pleasure to meet you, Aline."

"And you, Margaret."

Ms. Span departed.

"Mom, we were wondering," said Henrietta, "if we could invite our other friend to study with us. She's in kindergarten. She was sick yesterday at school, and Gary and I helped her."

"Sick?" said her mother. "Is she contagious?"

"Sick from headaches, like me. Can we invite her?"

"Your father will be home soon, dinner is on the way, and I'm still finishing up some work . . ." Her mother trailed off when she realized how nice it was that Henrietta was gaining some friends. "Oh, all right," she said.

Henrietta and Gary returned to Henrietta's room, where they looked up Rose's number on the school network. Rose's mother answered and agreed that Rose's father could bring their daughter over and that, of course, he would enjoy seeing Henrietta's house and meeting her mom.

●·· ··●

They waited out on the sidewalk. Traffic crawled through the lilac haze, and they thought about the street in the past. Henrietta wondered if the red bricks had been buried under the asphalt. Gary wondered about the trees, and the giant stump—were the roots still growing underground, even now? The thought made him feel claustrophobic.

"I wonder what kind of car Rose's dad drives," said Henrietta. "Hey, did you see any cars when we looked out the attic window?"

"I didn't," said Gary. Just then, a small puff of exhaust blew a candy-wrapper past their feet. Gary bent somewhat reflexively to grab it, and when he straightened he saw two figures approaching along the sidewalk.

He squinted at them. "There they are," he said. "They're . . . *walking?*"

Rose and her father were indeed walking along the sidewalk, holding hands. Henrietta and Gary had scarcely ever seen adults walking anywhere except to and from their cars.

"On foot they're going faster than the traffic," Henrietta observed.

Rose's father was tall, slender, and darker-skinned than Rose, with curly black hair. He wore khaki cotton pants, which Henrietta could identify easily because they weren't shiny like most pants. Rose was wearing the same wool shirt Henrietta had seen her in the other day.

"You *walked*," Gary said as they arrived.

"It's good to meet you both," said Rose's father. His voice struck Henrietta as quite friendly. "Rose's mother told me you looked after Rose during her headache. That was very kind."

"I'm Henrietta, and this is Gary," said Henrietta. "Come in and meet my mom." She opened the front door and ushered everyone in.

Henrietta's mother was waiting in the sitting room, and she stood as the guests entered.

"It's nice to meet you," said Rose's father. "Call me Sid."

"Aline," said Henrietta's mother. "Won't you have a seat? Sorry about this old house. We're planning to move soon."

"Oh, I like old houses," said Rose's father. "Some things about them can be quite nice."

"You'll have to tell me what those things are," said Henrietta's mother with a laugh.

"I don't think you've met my daughter, Rose," said Sid.

"It's nice to meet you, Rose," said Henrietta's mother. "Are you in kindergarten? You seem a little young, I must say."

"I'm old," said Rose.

"Can I make everyone some instant lavender tea?" She gestured toward the kitchen.

"Thank you, that would be nice," said Sid.

"Um, can we go study now?" Henrietta blurted.

●●·····●●

As soon as they entered Henrietta's room and closed the door, they saw that Henrietta and Gary had accidentally left the chair sitting atop her desk.

Henrietta winced at the oversight. They would need to be more careful.

"Why is that up there?" said Rose.

"Rose," said Henrietta, "we're going to show you a secret. But you have to promise not to tell."

Rose, used to keeping secrets, nodded.

Henrietta gave Gary an expectant look, and he clambered onto the chair, opened the trapdoor, and pulled himself up easily, as if he'd been doing it for months.

"An attic," Rose observed, intrigued but not apparently amazed.

"When we're up there," said Henrietta, "you have to be quiet so our parents don't hear."

Henrietta was going to help Rose, because she seemed too small to climb up by herself, but to her surprise Rose zipped onto the desk and the chair, jumped to catch the frame of the attic door, and pulled herself inside, all in about half the time it normally took Henrietta, who followed as quickly as she could, feeling oafish in comparison.

The wild housecat stood and stretched on the couch as they entered.

"Rose," said Henrietta, "this is a wild housecat. I found it up here." Then to the cat she said, "This is my other friend, Rose."

The cat curled its tail over its feet and yawned.

"What's its name?" said Rose.

"I . . . don't know!" said Henrietta, a little taken aback.

"Yeah, we *should* call it something other than just 'the cat,'" said Gary.

"What's a good name for a wild housecat?" said Henrietta.

"Is it a boy or a girl?" said Rose.

"I don't know that, either," said Henrietta. "My grandpa said it's supposed to be extinct, but I don't know much else."

They all looked at the cat. It did not announce its gender.

"We should pick something that would work either way," said Henrietta.

"How about Mister Lady?" said Rose.

Gary and Henrietta grinned. "Perfect!" said Gary.

"Do you mind if we call you Mister Lady?" Henrietta asked.

The cat narrowed its eyes a little and cocked its head. It didn't seem thrilled. "It doesn't *not* like it," said Gary. He turned away from the couch and walked over toward the windows.

"If you ever want us to call you something different," said Henrietta, "just . . . let us know." That cat perhaps nodded a little bit, though Henrietta couldn't be sure. It lay down and curled up on the couch, closing its eyes.

"I've only been up here a few times," said Henrietta to Rose. "I don't know what any of the stuff back there is." She gestured past the bookcases at the many shadowy objects behind in the deep recesses. "It used to belong to my grandmother."

"Rose, come look out the windows," said Gary. Rose and Henrietta joined him.

On the street below, a woman with a cart full of fruit gestured toward her apples, several adults on the sidewalk carried on an animated discussion, and a group of children skipped past, joking with one another and playing tag. One of them jumped onto the giant stump and ran across it.

"I don't understand," said Rose.

"This is the past," said Gary. "That's what the street outside used to look like here, a long time ago."

"We don't know why we can see it, though," said Henrietta. She and Gary were waiting for the moment when Rose understood, and became as thrilled as they had been. Instead of seeming surprised, though, Rose said, "Their school gets out a little after ours." Gary and Henrietta saw that the children walking past below were all carrying books and book bags.

Henrietta glanced over at the couch then to see Mister Lady hop down from it and limp over with some difficulty to stand next to the three of them, looking down on the old town with a gaze that seemed somehow sad. After a moment, the cat put a paw gently up against the glass.

"I think Mister Lady might be from there," Rose speculated. "Maybe she's wishing she could go back."

Henrietta glanced at the couch again, and noticed something. The cobweb she'd earlier placed there was gone. "Hey!" she said to Mister Lady. "Did you eat that?"

Mister Lady limped back over to the couch and laboriously climbed onto it, her injured leg dangling awkwardly. She looked at the three of them, and her expression, if Henrietta interpreted it correctly, said *It's about time you noticed.*

Henrietta said, "I've been trying to figure out what it eats! I was reading this—" she pointed to the *Bestiary*, open on the coffee table. She flipped to the page on wild housecats as Gary and Rose looked on.

"That's a drawing of one!" said Gary, pointing at the illustration in amazement. "Right there, like in a textbook, like it's real!"

"It is real," said Henrietta. "And read the entry." She gestured to the cursive.

"I can't read cursive," said Rose.

Henrietta looked to Gary.

"Uh . . ." he said. His eyes darted around suddenly, evasively, and he backed away from the book. He turned partway toward the trapdoor, but stopped. A grim determination settled on his features, and he faced his friends. "I have to tell you both something," he said. "My secret." He looked up at the rafters and then down at his shoes. "It's . . . well . . ." He hesitated, and seemed to brace himself. "I can't read," he said finally. He spat the words.

In the midst of the strangeness of the attic, this really was a surprise. Henrietta had half expected Gary to admit that he could make things float with his mind, or become invisible. It took her a moment to absorb his admission.

"But you're the teacher's kid," she said. Gary's face turned scarlet, and he glanced at Rose. Henrietta clapped one hand over her mouth—she'd been so shocked, she'd forgotten that this was also a secret.

"It's okay," Gary sighed. "Rose, my mom is our teacher." Rose nodded, still somehow immune to surprise.

"But you pass the practice tests!" Henrietta protested. "And the Competency Exams! You're the best in class."

"I know how to *type*," said Gary. "I just can't read what I type."

"What about when we write compositions?"

"I ask my mom what it's going to be, and then I copy stuff the night before and memorize the letters."

"That seems harder than reading," said Henrietta.

"Well, it isn't," said Gary. "And don't tell my mom. If she knew, she'd ground me forever."

"You'd be Finished," said Henrietta.

"Yeah," said Gary. "But the thing is, too—" Now that he'd started talking, he wasn't about to stop. From the quickness with which the words spilled forth, it was obvious he'd wanted to confess this for a long time. "—I think I'd *like* being a garbage collector. I wouldn't have to fake anything anymore. And, and, actually . . ." Gary put his hand in his pocket and pulled it out to reveal a small, crumpled up piece of paper. He sat at the table and began to unfold it. "I kind of like garbage. I have a collection of it."

Henrietta and Rose stared at him as he continued to attentively smooth the small sheet.

"Trash?" said Henrietta.

"Interesting trash," said Gary. "Like this," he said. He finished smoothing out the little piece of paper. It was a sticky note which had the words henʀift and andi scrawled upon it.

"Where did you get that?" Henrietta and Rose said simultaneously. For the first time, Rose looked completely surprised.

"History Nutrition room trash can," said Gary. "I saw Henrietta throw it out, and I wondered what it was. I've looked at it for awhile. I think someone made a mistake on it. I think it says 'And and I.' I'm not sure," he admitted, still obviously embarrassed by his poor reading skills.

"Rose wrote it," said Henrietta.

"That movie was wrong," said Rose. "There's no one named Henrift Andi.

It was two people. Henrift and Andi."

"How do you know?"

"A book my dad read me," said Rose. "It said there were two people. They were scientists. A man and a woman."

"That's weird," said Henrietta. "Why would the movie be wrong?"

"I wish I could read," said Gary, folding the sticky note and returning it to his pocket.

"Well, we did tell my mom we'd study," said Henrietta.

Gary looked doubtful. "I'm pretty stupid," he said. "Maybe we could try later. Weren't you about to tell us something?"

Henrietta let the issue drop. She pointed at the *Bestiary*. "This says wild housecats eat cobwebs, and so I put a cobweb on the couch, and . . ."

"And Mister Lady ate it?" said Gary. "Let's get more!" There was a relieved note in his voice.

For the next several minutes, they forgot themselves in a flurry of gathering. Henrietta and Gary stayed close to the main area, both still a little nervous about being on their own. The dark lanes of old stuff behind the bookshelves, though full of magnificent cobwebs, seemed a bit scary. But this didn't deter Rose. The attic reminded her of home. The moment she'd arrived and taken a breath she smelled the wonderful rich pages of all the old books.

She went straight behind the bookcases, going far back into the dusty depths, where there were old dressers, tables, locked chests, stacked boxes, a record player, and many other fascinating antiques.

Encouraged by Rose's confidence, Henrietta and Gary ventured a little further as well, and soon the three of them had amassed a considerable ball of cobwebs, which they deposited next to Mister Lady on the couch. As the children watched, the cat batted the ball lightly with one velvet paw, sending it rolling a few inches across the cushion, and then looked up at them. Henrietta thought its expression might have said, *This could have been a little bigger, but thanks.*

"We should probably go back down," said Henrietta, "in case my mom comes to check."

She opened the trapdoor, and the three returned to her room. They heard Rose's father's voice from elsewhere in the house, and proceeded to the sitting room, where Henrietta's mother and he were conversing.

"We have instant lavender or instant peppermint," Henrietta's mother said.

Henrietta turned to Gary and Rose, and motioned for them to step back into the hall.

"They're *just* sitting down," she whispered. "That's what they were saying when we left!"

"I don't get it," said Gary.

"I don't think any time has passed," Henrietta said.

PART 2

Spike-Tailed Fish
and Flesh-Eating Worms

T ime passed—or didn't—happily for a few weeks after these many discoveries. Henrietta visited the attic twice each day: afternoons after school with Gary and Rose, and at night before bed, alone, when she changed Mister Lady's bandages. The wound was almost entirely healed, although for some reason it seemed reluctant to close completely.

Henrietta liked being in the attic at night. It reminded her of the evening she'd first discovered it, and she'd begun to enjoy being by herself. She found she could think more clearly, and she sometimes sat on the couch in silence with Mister Lady, not doing anything other than rolling the events of the day around in her head.

When the moon shone through the windows it brought a haunting glow to the little living room, the dusty bookshelves, and the deep interior. It was both eerie and beautiful.

•·· ··•

Afternoons when school finished, Rose, Gary, and Henrietta went up together. They'd spend hours talking, looking out the windows, reading old books, playing games, and studying. One afternoon Gary brought some of his most prized trash objects, which included a strip of fabric from an old chair that had an image of an acorn stitched on it, and a box from a brand of TV dinner that didn't exist anymore. Henrietta and Rose couldn't see exactly what Gary found so fascinating, but he spoke in low tones, saying, "Now *this* is of *particular* interest. . . ." before revealing a tan Styrofoam packing peanut. Henrietta began to wonder if maybe Gary really *should* let himself get Finished from school. If anyone would make a good garbage collector, it would be him.

Another afternoon, Rose surprised Henrietta and Gary when she arrived in the attic armed with linen thread, glue, a ruler, a razor, and a metal spike with a wooden handle, all of which she laid on the coffee table with great solemnity.

"What is all of this?" said Gary. "It looks dangerous. What's that?" He pointed to the spike.

"An awl," said Rose. "These are for repairing books. Like the *Bestiary*." She opened the front cover and showed Henrietta and Gary that the endpapers were partly unglued, and a tear had started down the hinge of the back cover.

"I didn't know books could be repaired," said Gary. "Isn't it more sensible to just get a new one?"

"A new *Bestiary*?" said Rose.

"Oh, right," said Gary. When it's irreplaceable, it makes sense to take care of it.

There followed a most illuminating conservation lecture in which Rose described the parts of a book, its materials, and common construction methods. Then she effected a simple repair of the *Bestiary*, much to the amazement of Henrietta and Gary. "My dad is better at it," she said.

"Where did he learn?" said Henrietta.

". . . Nowhere," said Rose. Further questioning produced only silence.

●•• ••●

Mister Lady grew increasingly active as days passed, often chasing after motes of dust in the main area. One afternoon Henrietta found a tuft of fur beside the couch, and concluded that the cat was also doing some hunting.

Through the windows, Henrietta, Gary, and Rose continued their fascination with the old world outside. Usually when they arrived they'd see the children coming home from school, but sometimes the two eras came unstuck from one another and they'd arrive to find midnight through the windows, or sunrise.

Whenever the sun was out, so were people, crossing the boulevard on errands, chatting on street-side benches, selling groceries and other goods from carts. One afternoon a whole picnic took place atop the gigantic stump, and thirty people ate and drank there. Occasionally, a car passed, strange and large, and people stopped what they were doing to look. Cars were a curiosity.

At sunset, a man would stroll the boulevard bearing a long metal stick with a flame at the end, lighting the streetlamps. A real flame burned in every one, flickering and casting wavering shadows along the trunks of the maple trees.

●•• ••●

All three children spent considerable time reading up in the attic, even Gary. One of the things that had always kept him from reading was that he couldn't see the point. Why read when you could learn from TV or the radio, or ask a computer, or your cell phone? But in the attic, reading was quite helpful.

One afternoon, while exploring behind the bookshelves, Gary happened upon a large glass jar full of thick, glaucous liquid. Floating in it was some kind of preserved creature. He carefully picked up the jar and carried it out past a pile of luggage, an old dresser, a sewing table, and the bookcases to the living room, where he placed it on the coffee table.

Henrietta jumped when she saw it. The thing looked like a gray bird, but it was covered in scales like a fish. It sloshed gently back and forth in the cloudy solution, which Gary's transport had agitated.

If Gary had seen something like this at school he would have taken a picture of it with his phone, and the phone would have told him what he was looking at. Or he could have spoken a few descriptive words, like "Part bird, part fish," and his phone would have sorted some search results based on those keywords.

And, indeed, Gary did produce his phone with the intent of taking a picture . . . but the phone was dead. "It's broken," he said, shaking it a little.

"That happened up here to me, too," said Henrietta. She took out her own phone. The screen was blank.

"Rose, does yours work?" said Henrietta. Rose, over by the windows, was watching a group of children kick an empty can along the brick street.

"I don't have one," she said.

"I forgot," said Henrietta. "Why don't your parents get you one? What if there's an emergency?"

Rose shrugged. She came over to look at Henrietta's phone.

"It's like at my house," said Rose.

"Your house?" said Henrietta.

Rose's mouth snapped shut so fast her teeth clicked.

"What is it, Rose?" said Gary, sensing her hesitation.

"Nothing." Rose sat by the coffee table and looked into the glass jar at the strange preserved creature.

"Does your house have a lot of books in it?" said Henrietta. "Is that why you know how to repair them?"

Rose continued to look silently at the creature. At the end of its tail was a long, threateningly curved hook.

"Let's see if it's in the *Bestiary*." She slid the book toward Gary. "Do you want to try it?"

"You know I can't," he said, scowling.

"I didn't mean it like that," said Henrietta. "I was just thinking—it doesn't matter how long it takes when we're up here. If you want to try."

"I guess that's true," said Gary. He brightened a little. The lack of time pressure made the situation seem a little more encouraging. He opened the Bestiary, and Henrietta and Rose sat on either side of him. Even Mister Lady approached to watch.

"This might be kind of hard," said Henrietta, "since we don't know what it's called."

"But there are pictures," said Gary, flipping through the brittle old pages. "Let's just look for it."

"I didn't think of that," said Henrietta.

"Because you can read," said Gary, smiling. It took a while, but they finally found an illustration that resembled the creature in the jar.

Henrietta read the title silently. She looked at Gary.

"Do you know how to sound things out?" she asked.

"A little," said Gary.

"That's a Q," said Rose, pointing at the first letter.

"Kw . . ." Gary said. "And the next letter is a *U*, then an *A* . . . *A* is like 'apple,' right?"

"It depends," said Henrietta.

"That's what I hate about reading!" said Gary, instantly exasperated. "It's like they make it hard on purpose."

If the alphabet had been invented in the Addition, all *A*s would probably sound like the *A* in *apple*. In the Addition, streets ran on a grid, and the houses were identical. The "number one" at one restaurant was the same as the "number one" at every other restaurant, and it would only make sense to have an equally regular alphabet.

But the alphabet was irregular. The rules all had exceptions, and some of the exceptions even had exceptions. The alphabet was like the Old City. The pitched roof of Henrietta's house, for instance, was an exception to the rule of flat roofs. Maybe Henrietta's house should be remodeled to have a flat roof, and maybe the alphabet should be remodeled so all the *A*s sounded like the *A* in *apple*.

But if Henrietta's house had a flat roof, this story wouldn't have happened. Mister Lady would not have been able to sneak in. Mysterious jars would not be hidden away among strange artifacts. There would be no windows looking into the past. The alphabet's different *As* had caused Gary some problems, but the attic was giving him the time he needed to sort them out.

●·· ··●

With occasional guidance from Henrietta, Gary and Rose sounded out the text of the description of the quaverly (a word in which the *A* sounds like the *A* in "*Safe*"). Here's what they read:

A beach-dwelling, nocturnal Carnivore, Quaverly live in Schools of up to one hundred thousand individuals. Roosting and sleeping during the Day under driftwood logs, suspended by a chitinous Hook, this placid Creature drops from its roost at night to the Sand, and enters tidal pools and shallows to provender upon Shrimp, Sand Fleas, and other small Fauna.

Though edible, Quaverly is rarely prepared owing to its bitter Taste, want of Meat, and nearly imperturbable Hide. However, its Abundance has made it useful to Humans in times of severe Lack—especially in Winter-time, when its Population swells after the Autumnal mating season.

— Henrift

They didn't figure it all out at once. Even Henrietta had to use the dictionary here and there for words like *chitinous* (hard, like a beetle shell) and *provender* (to feed). When they finished, Gary slumped. "That was the hardest thing I've ever done."

"Way harder than what we read in school," said Henrietta.

Rose peered at the page. "What's that?" she asked, pointing to the word "Henrift" at the very end.

"That's the name of the person who wrote this entry," said Henrietta. "Look here." She flipped to the front of the book. "See, *Aristotle Alcott*, that's the *A.A.* at the end of some of the entries. I wonder if this *Henrift* is the same one from History in school."

"I can't believe they wrote this whole thing out by *hand*," said Gary.

"My grandfather said it was made before people typed. He has a newer *Bestiary*, too. It's old, but not this old. It's typed, and it's longer, because they'd learned more."

"It's weird, as we flipped through," said Gary. "I've never heard of any of the animals."

They looked again, skimming past the illustrations. The diversity of pictured life was fascinating: mesmer vole, airship whale, springer, tail fox, candlefly, statium, pulchritude hound, pif, greater pif, paf. . . .

"I guess they're all extinct," said Henrietta. "That's what my grandfather said about wild housecats, too."

As if on cue, Mister Lady took a brief experimental swipe at the quaverly in the jar, as if to ascertain whether or not it might be chased.

"I think Mister Lady is a girl," Rose said abruptly.

Henrietta and Gary agreed, though they weren't sure why.

●•• ••●

At school, the lessons slowly progressed day to day and the Competency Exam grew inexorably nearer. Gary continued to cheat as always, and so maintained his position at the top of the class. Henrietta never cheated, but she found her work improving considerably, even though school seemed more awful and boring than ever. She wasn't sure why she was doing better. Partly, it was that she didn't want to miss her bus after school, because she could go into the attic with her friends. Partly it was because she was feeling happier than she had in a long time.

And partly, it was because her reading skills were improving. Every day, she learned new words, and encountered more difficult sentences, and she waded through them with increasing expertise. In fact, she was becoming quite an excellent reader, and she had an excellent memory for new words, which seemed to stick in her head like flies to flypaper. She was ensnaring herself a superlative vocabulary.

●·· ··●

After school on the day before the Competency Exam, while Henrietta ducked around with Rose behind the book cases collecting cobwebs, they ran across a book whose title caught Henrietta's eye: *Early Town*. She slid it from the shelf and returned to the couch, laying her harvest of webs next to Mister Lady. She opened the book and turned to the title page.

EARLY TOWN:
A Book of Records Including Maps and Services

The next page, printed in black, blue, and red ink, folded out to become twice as wide as the book. The legend at the top read CITY MAP. Henrietta had never seen a map before, except in the movie *Watch Out for Pirates*, when some buccaneers had used one to find buried treasure.

Gary and Rose looked over Henrietta's shoulder at the folded-out page. Mister Lady approached as well, curious as she always was whenever anyone read something. She often peered over their shoulders while they waded through the old books, and Henrietta had begun to wonder about it—maybe the cat really could read.

"What is it?" Gary asked.

"A map," said Henrietta.

"Like in *Watch Out for Pirates*?"

"But not a treasure map," said Henrietta. "Just a regular map. It shows how the city used to be."

"I don't get it," said Gary.

"Pretend we're floating over the buildings," said Henrietta. She pointed at a straight red line. "This is a road."

"And that's a river," said Rose, pointing to a meandering blue line.

"And the squares are buildings?" said Gary. "We don't really need these anymore I guess, since your car or your phone just tells you."

"This seems kind of better, though," said Henrietta.

"It seems complicated," said Gary.

"But when your car tells you, you don't really know where you're going."

"Yeah, I guess so," said Gary. "If the phone says 'turn left' . . . I can see how a map is better."

"Also, I like how it looks," said Henrietta. "It's like a painting."

"If I found it in the trash, I'd definitely keep it," said Gary.

"It doesn't show what's here now," said Rose.

"It's what used to be, back then, I bet," said Henrietta, gesturing out the attic windows.

It took some puzzling out because the map contained many streets, houses, and streams. Labels for everything were crammed in at different angles, but they eventually found a street with the same name as theirs: *Boardwalk*. Strangely, it was right at the far left edge of the map, like it was the last street, period.

"It looks like we're on the edge of the world," said Henrietta. "I wonder what's beyond it."

"The Addition," said Rose.

"But why isn't it on here?"

"It wasn't built yet."

For a few moments the children contemplated the fact that the city they lived in, every building and every street, hadn't always existed.

"I want to know everything that happened between then and now," said Gary.

"I wonder how long ago it was," said Henrietta.

"If any of those people are still alive," said Rose.

The three of them walked to the windows and looked down at the narrow brick road. At the moment, the boulevard was nearly empty. Two young men sat on the edge of the giant stump, arguing earnestly and passing a steaming thermos back and forth between them.

"They should see their street now," said Gary. "I wonder if they'd like it."

"Maybe some of them *have* seen it both ways," said Henrietta. "Like my grandparents."

"I want to tell those people not to chop down the trees," said Gary. He looked out at the soaring boughs and wished he could somehow prevent them from disappearing. The leaves were full of the gold and red of autumn, and some had fallen in stiff breezes and littered the ground, skittering here and there along the bricks and across the great stump.

"Hey, look!" said Henrietta, pointing high into the branches of one of the trees. "There!" She kept pointing, following the form as it moved from branch to branch within the deep orange foliage. Because of its orange fur, it was tough to see. "It's . . . I think it's a wild housecat!"

Suddenly, from behind them, Mister Lady leaped down from the couch. Before Henrietta could turn, the cat was beside them, pressing her front paws against the windowsill. Her green eyes were wide.

"I see it!" said Gary.

"Me too," said Rose.

The cat was huge, a tabby even larger than Mister Lady. It left the shadows for a moment to run across a thick branch right by the windows. As it passed, Mister Lady let out a long, plaintive meow. She pawed at the glass, but the tabby neither saw nor heard her. In another instant it reentered the shadows of the heavy foliage, and disappeared as it leaped effortlessly on its long legs from one tree to another and continued down the boulevard.

Mister Lady stared after it, her eyes seeking this way and that for another glimpse. Finally she turned and walked back to the couch. Her limp was nearly gone now, but her gait was slow, dejected.

"I think she really is from out there," said Gary.

"I wonder how much longer she'll stay here," said Henrietta. "She's almost better." This was a tough thought, because none of the three wanted to lose Mister Lady, who was as much a part of their shared friendship as anyone.

They looked down as a few more schoolchildren ran by, chasing after leaves and playing. Seeing them turned Henrietta's thoughts back toward class. "Gary, do you think you'll cheat on the Competency Exam tomorrow?" she asked.

"I'm just not good enough yet to do it on my own," he replied. "What if I got Finished? I'd never see you guys again. Say, do *you* want to cheat?" he asked. "I could help you."

"Actually, I'm kind of looking forward to it," said Henrietta, "after all the practice we've done up here."

"These books are different from the computer questions," said Gary.

"It's all reading, though," said Henrietta. "People have been doing it since forever."

●·· ··●

That night, as Henrietta changed Mister Lady's bandages and sterilized the wound, she made a disturbing discovery. In the near-darkness of the attic, she shone her flashlight on the cat's injured leg and saw several small, white worms crawling.

"*Ugh!*" She simultaneously recoiled from them and reached out to brush them off. Mister Lady wrenched away and leapt onto a bookshelf several feet above Henrietta's head. It was the first such leap Henrietta had ever seen the cat make. The ease and strength of the jump was astounding, and Henrietta felt a small resurgence of the fear she'd felt when she and Mister Lady first met.

"I'm sorry," said Henrietta. "Please come down."

The sight of the worms squirmed awfully in her brain. How could that have happened? She'd been so careful to keep the wound clean. Her eyes fell on the *Bestiary*, which lay as always atop the glass coffee table.

Henrietta flipped to the index. Scanning through, she noticed an entry for "Worm—Flesh-Eating."

Worm, Flesh-Eating:

Though disturbing on first encounter, and often erroneously associated with Uncleanliness and Disease, the Flesh-Eating Worm is beneficial to Humans. The presence of Flesh-Eating Worms in a Wound is indicative of the Restoration of an Injury to Health, as the creatures consume only dead and diseased Flesh. Their attentions are a boon to Healing. It is most unfortunate that many souls benighted by Ignorance view these worms incorrectly as the Cause and Continuation of the Necrosis they in fact hasten to eradicate.
—Recorded and observed by E. S.

It went against good sense, but somehow it also made sense. Henrietta turned to the bookcase, from which Mr. Lady glared down. "All right," she said. "I'll leave them. But it's gross."

The Competency Exam

After weeks of practice tests, detention, and homework, the morning of the Competency Exam arrived to find Henrietta waiting at the bus stop for Gary, bursting to inform him about flesh-eating worms. Gary was a good person to tell disgusting things to because he could be relied upon to make revolted faces. Hopefully the diversion would take both of their minds off the test for a few minutes.

Unfortunately, Gary was also the kind of person to show up a little late for things, and he trudged up just as the bus arrived. As it slowed for the children, the cars behind it began honking.

"MIRACLE MEDICAL WISHES ALL STUDENTS GOOD LUCK ON THEIR COMPETENCY EXAMS!"

"GOT AN A ON YOUR EXAM? CELEBRATE WITH A SKIPPING-STONE PHONE FROM TINCAN TELECOMM!"

Henrietta said hello to Gary, and he said hello back, but neither could hear the other over the racket. They strapped themselves into their seats, the blue warning lights turned off, and the yellow safety light turned on. As the bus picked up speed and the Honk Ads diminished, Henrietta said, "Are you nervous?"

"I know all the questions," said Gary. "I'm ready."

"You really just ask your mom?"

"Yeah."

"Do you feel guilty about it?" Henrietta couldn't imagine taking similar advantage, were she in his position.

"Maybe a little," he said, shrugging as well as he could in his harness. "But I also think the tests are dumb."

"I never thought about it that way," said Henrietta. She always felt bad about her grades, but what if grades were the problem, and not her?

Suddenly, something happened that didn't normally happen.

From the empty seat in front of them, a head rose up and peered back over the headrest. The face had a tiny nose, a weak chin, and thin yellow hair partly covering a tall forehead. It flickered briefly as its pale yellow eyes focused on the two of them.

The bus's security system didn't respond to the infraction: No lights went on or off, and the engine didn't shut down.

Gary gasped. "You!" he said.

Henrietta froze. Her heart gulped.

"Get away!" said Gary. He wrestled against his restraints, but after his encounter with the driver weeks back, the school district had retrofitted the buses with automated seat belts. The children were trapped.

The thing's mouth opened into a round hole with a guttering yellow light glowing up from its pink throat. Its voice leaked out, slow and scratchy, like a recording. Its lips didn't move to form the words. "WHERE DO YOU GO?" it said.

Henrietta wanted to look over at Gary, but her eyes wouldn't respond to her urging. "WHERE DO YOU GO?" the voice came again. Its inflections were exactly the same as the first time. The thing brought an arm up over the back of the seat and one long, waxen index finger reached toward Gary.

"Don't!" Henrietta whispered.

The finger lightly tapped Gary's forehead, and the creature winked out, disappearing like a switched-off light.

"I need my medicine," said Gary, his voice trembling and small. He was pale and sweating. He squeezed his eyes shut.

Henrietta racked her brain, trying to figure out if there was any way to get out of her straps. Finally, she did the only thing she could think of: she screamed.

●·· ··●

Once they arrived at school, a crumpled Gary was whisked to Ms. Morse's office by the bus duty supervisor. Henrietta, after a brief trip to the principal's office to receive a Behavioral Citation and a lecture about Being Disruptive on the Bus, had to proceed straight to class to take the Competency Exam.

It was no longer practice. This was what they'd all been preparing for. Statistics from this test would be tabulated for all districts, schools, classes, and students. Schools could lose funding, teachers could lose jobs, and students could be classified as At Risk or even Finished. Henrietta entered the room and sat silently at the back, next to Gary's empty chair.

At the front, Ms. Span stood and silently watched her nervous students. She was dressed in a black sweater and black slacks, scrupulously devoid of any piece of lint. Her black hair was pulled back into a perfect bun, and her normally thick eyebrows were plucked into precise arcs. Despite her severe appearance, Henrietta could tell she was worried. Not only was the exam itself stressful, and her best student sidelined, but that student was her son, and she couldn't go visit him to see how he was doing.

When Ms. Span had everyone's undivided attention, she spoke. "Read every question twice," she said, speaking slowly and articulating carefully. "Be fast and accurate. Never leave a blank. It is vitally important that you do well today, for yourself, and for me, and for the school. Failure will have real consequences, up to and including being Finished." She paused. "Don't be nervous," she added. She smiled nervously. "Don't be anxious."

The class hung on her every word. Finally, she donned her reading glasses and spent a few moments tilting them back and forth on her nose to make sure they were perfectly straight. Meanwhile, in homes and workplaces all across the Addition, parents held their cell phones before them in sweating hands, watching anxiously for news.

Ms. Span sat at her terminal. "Get ready," she said as the clock approached the hour. In seconds, every student in every school in every district everywhere would be presented with their first short response question; the same question for everyone, every child responding in parallel with every other child.

The clock turned. "Begin!" said Ms. Span as everyone's screen went momentarily blank, and then lit up with the prompt.

WHERE DO YOU GO?

"Don't start!" said Ms. Span, her voice shrill. She typed at her terminal. "It must be a glitch. . . ." She frowned. "No, this is it. This is the question! Go!"

"What does it mean?" said one student.

"It doesn't matter," said Ms. Span. "Just answer it!"

"But what do we say?"

"Where you go! Write about where you go!"

The students wrote, though the question was unlike the ones they were accustomed to. Henrietta studied her own screen a little longer than everyone else, half expecting the face of the yellow-haired creature to loom up and look back at her. Her cursor blinked impatiently. Time was clicking by. She slouched a bit in concentration, and began.

I NEVER WEARY OF PERAMBULATING TO LURMY'S, BECAUSE IT ALWAYS HAS HIGH-QUALITY, AFFORDABLE PROVENDER.

As she typed, the word *perambulating* (which she knew meant to walk about leisurely) showed up underlined in red—a mistake. She had learned the word from the *Bestiary*, though, and had even looked it up in the attic's dusty dictionary, so she knew she was using it correctly. Another red underline appeared under *provender*, but she kept writing—there was no time for second thoughts.

Soon, the two minutes were up, and the terminal froze. The data was sent to the district for processing. "Don't worry about how you did," Ms. Span chirped from the front. "It's too late. Math is next!"

Many of the students looked mystified and nervous as the seconds ticked down toward the appearance of the first multiple-choice math question.

"Remember, C is most common," said Ms. Span quietly. Henrietta looked up at her, a little surprised. Giving directions after the test began was against the rules. The class's composition grades must not have been good. The first math question appeared.

20 + 5 =
A) 25
B) 25
C) 25
D) 25

"Don't respond!" Ms. Span said. She typed for a few moments and watched her screen. "That's the question!" she called out. "Answer and move on!"

"But which is it?" said one student.

"Just *answer*," barked Ms. Span.

Henrietta clicked C), and her computer made a soft *ding* sound to indicate that she'd answered correctly. The same *ding* sounded around her as other students submitted their answers, and here and there a *clunk* rang out, the sound of a garbage can's contents being dumped into a truck. Henrietta saw some students sitting with their eyes squeezed shut. The next problem appeared. This one was fill-in-the-blank.

30 - 10 =

Henrietta typed "20" and submitted it. To her surprise, though, her computer responded with a heart-stopping *clunk*.

Around her, other computers *clunk*ed. At the front of the room, Ms. Span's neat bun had begun to come loose. A strand of hair hung in front of her face, and her reading glasses were askew. She typed madly at her terminal.

The next question appeared.

20 - 5 =

"Don't respond!" she said, typing furiously. "All right, everyone. *Silence.* Pay attention. Math is different now. Minus means plus now. When you see minus, think *plus.*"

"But—" began several students.

"*Minus means plus!*" Ms. Span shouted. Her voice cracked.

Henrietta looked at the problem. All right, then. "20 - 5" should be "20 + 5." Henrietta entered "25." Her computer *ding*ed—correct. Around her, other computers *ding*ed, although some *clunk*ed. Some of the students were evidently having difficulty thinking of "minus" as "plus."

The next problem:

10 + 10 =

"Ms. Span, if minus is plus, is plus minus?" said Bernard Faust, a large boy whose scores were generally near the bottom of the class. He sat next to Clarence Frederick, and both of them were shooting worried glances all around, unsure what to do.

"I don't know," said Ms. Span. Her voice had become very calm. "Answer and move on," she said. She held up her arms, like someone making a plea for help.

Henrietta typed "20" and submitted it. *Ding.*

●·· ··●

That was how the remainder of the math portion worked out. Minus had become plus, but plus was still plus. In other words, the test contained no subtraction problems. Once the students got the hang of it, Ms. Span seemed to recover some degree of her composure, straightening her glasses and running a hand over her black hair to smooth it. The exam ended and the bell rang for History and Nutrition.

"Everyone, Mason the bus supervisor is waiting outside to escort you today, while I stay here to collate the results."

The students stood, some a little shakily, others wiping tears from red cheeks, and walked silently out the door. Henrietta was preparing to follow when Ms. Span's voice stopped her in her tracks. "Henrietta." She did not sound pleased.

Henrietta approached the front as the last few students exited.

"You did well on the math today," Ms. Span said, removing her reading glasses.

"Thank you," said Henrietta. She could tell this wasn't going to be good news.

"But your composition. It was . . . inexcusable." Ms. Span turned her computer screen to face Henrietta and displayed Henrietta's essay, with FAIL written across the top. Below, the many words Henrietta had learned in the attic were underlined in red, one after the other.

"What is this supposed to mean?" said Ms. Span, donning her glasses again to peer at the screen and then removing them as if the sight caused her physical pain. "Why are you making up words, Henrietta?"

"I didn't," said Henrietta.

Ms. Span shook her head. "This essay decreased our class's aggregated statistic by two percent."

"I'm sorry, Ms. Span," said Henrietta.

"Henrietta, this essay, plus your Behavioral Citation this morning, has forced me to classify you as At Risk for the remainder of the year. If you perform like this again, you will be Finished."

"But—" said Henrietta.

"If I don't declare you At Risk, the whole class will suffer from having your scores included. Do you want that?"

"No," said Henrietta.

Ms. Span sighed. She massaged her plucked eyebrows with one hand. "Henrietta, I don't want to do it. I like you. Gary likes you. And I want to help you."

"I understand," said Henrietta, numbly. She wasn't really following the conversation anymore. Her mind had stopped at the words At Risk.

"We'll get through it if we commit to working hard. Gary will help you, too, I'm sure."

"Okay," said Henrietta. She looked up at the wall clock above, and observed the seconds clicking past.

"If you'd like to visit him at the nurse's office, Henrietta, I'll release you from History and Nutrition today. Ms. Morse just sent me a message that he's recovering."

"Thank you, Ms. Span."

Henrietta entered the hallway with her stomach clenched in a knot. Detention she could handle, but At Risk was something else entirely. Just a step away from a lifetime in a dingy apartment in the crime-ridden Old City, collecting garbage. A step from never seeing her friends again. She blinked furiously and wiped away shameful tears as she walked to Ms. Morse's office.

Her cell phone rang, and her mother's name appeared on the screen. She knew she should answer, but she didn't. Once it stopped ringing, it rang again—her father. By now they would both have received the news that she'd been reclassified.

When she opened the door to the infirmary, Ms. Morse was behind her desk, and wasn't surprised to see her.

"Rose is already with him," she said, gesturing.

Henrietta entered the recovery room. Gary lay on a cot, curled up with his hands loosely covering his face. He looked small. Rose sat across from him. "He'll be all right," she said as Henrietta sat next to her. They watched Gary's still form for awhile. "Rose, I'm At Risk," said Henrietta. "My parents are going to ground me forever. You probably shouldn't come over today."

"I'm sorry," said Rose. Her small face was full of sympathy, which made Henrietta feel a little better.

●•• ••●

Henrietta's Behavioral Citation had also earned her detention, during which she typed out a long list of District-Approved Vocabulary words provided by Ms. Span that included terms such as *bucket*, *grunt*, and *rug*. By the end, Henrietta had missed her bus and had to call her mother.

Her parents were both in the car when it arrived, which was almost unheard of. They received her with disappointed faces, told her she was grounded, supplied many unpleasant scenarios of her future life that would occur if she were Finished, and emphasized the importance of using District-Approved Vocabulary, glancing at Ms. Span's report recommendations on their phones as they spoke. Henrietta wished she could shrink into nothing. As her parents lectured, she dropped her chin to her chest.

When they arrived home, dinner was served in near-silence, and her father curtly assured Henrietta that she would get no dessert. Other grim facts were aired:

— The amount of money Henrietta's father lost by coming home early.

— The exact layout of the tiny, rat-infested Old City apartment where Henrietta would spend the rest of her days as a garbage collector, which did not feature a private bathroom.

— The shame that would be heaped forever upon the name of Gad-Fly if Henrietta were to become Finished.

Henrietta nodded when it seemed appropriate. Everything had piled on top of everything until she felt nothing. Finally, she was sent to her room to think about what she'd done. As soon as she arrived there, she climbed past the unseeing eye of the still-broken BedCam into the attic.

A luxuriant, greenish full moon shone through the large windows, reflecting perfectly in the glass top of the coffee table. The couch, ornamented with brocades of deep shadow, looked like a stone sculpture in the pale light.

On it Mister Lady reclined casually, reading *Early Town*, turning a page with a single sharp claw.

Henrietta froze when she saw this, and Mister Lady looked up abruptly. It was obvious she hadn't been expecting Henrietta at this moment.

"I'm sorry," said Henrietta. "I didn't mean to interrupt. I just can't do *anything* right."

The black pupils of the cat's green eyes were so large Henrietta felt swallowed by them. Mister Lady dropped the page, stood, and leaped easily to the top of a nearby bookcase, from which she looked down at Henrietta.

"I'm sorry," said Henrietta again. She felt like she should leave, but couldn't bear to go back down. Everything was too terrible.

When she blinked, she must have missed something. She must have because suddenly Mister Lady was gone. The place she'd just occupied atop the bookcase was empty.

"Hello?" said Henrietta quietly. There was no response. The silence of the attic was oppressive.

After wearying herself with searching, Henrietta descended back to her bedroom. The day could scarcely get worse. She shoved her feet and arms into the legs and sleeves of her polyester pajamas and slipped under her bedcovers. Disheartened, she fell asleep almost immediately, retreating from it all.

●·· ··●

It seemed like the end of an awful day, but it wasn't over yet. The world didn't stop turning just because Henrietta had gone to sleep.

At that moment, a massive, yellow truck turned onto the street outside of her house, blocking both northbound lanes of traffic. A yellow car followed it at a walking pace. A worker emerged from the passenger side of the car with a can of spray paint in one hand, and made marks on the road—numbers and symbols of obscure meaning.

Behind the yellow car drove a yellow van with a hole in its roof, through which protruded a tall swiveling platform where a worker stood, holding a large remote control covered with buttons. When the van approached a stoplight, the worker pushed a few buttons on the control, and the light went out.

Behind the yellow van drove another yellow truck, this one dropping saw-horses at intersections. Each sawhorse featured two bright yellow, flashing lights with a sign between that read: ROAD CLOSED. Eventually, this caravan of north-bound vehicles passed an identical caravan traveling southbound. After they passed one another, the street was empty.

For the first time in many years, there was silence on Henrietta's block.

The Department of Insta-Structure

The next morning, after a depressing breakfast of cornslaw and further remonstrances from both of her parents, Henrietta left the house to find Gary waiting outside. "Look!" he said, pointing to the street.

It was empty. There was no layer of smog curling on the ground. No horns blared. No engines rumbled. Henrietta stepped onto the sidewalk, looking up and down the street. Several blocks distant, she saw some cross-traffic out past the ROAD CLOSED signs. She scratched her head and turned to Gary. "How are you feeling?" she asked. She hadn't talked to him since his headache.

Instead of answering, Gary took a few comical steps out into the road and did a little dance. He waved his arms, jiggling them like rubber bands. "I just ran across to your house!" he said.

"Don't stand out there," said Henrietta. "The cars could come back." She looked up the street nervously.

"Oh, right," said Gary.

As they walked to the bus stop, Gary's levity diminished. He grabbed Henrietta's hand when they arrived. "I'm scared," he said. "I hope the bus doesn't come."

"Me, too," said Henrietta.

They hoped in vain. The crowded bus arrived, and they reluctantly boarded.

No cars honked in annoyance, and no targeted advertisements were deployed.

"Let's sit somewhere different," said Gary quietly.

They buckled into a pair of seats a few rows further back than usual. Gary closed his eyes.

●·· ··●

Not long after Henrietta departed for school, her mother Aline sat at the living room computer and checked her mail.

The first thing she saw was an advertisement for a Halloween trick-or-treating event at a nearby mall. Aline didn't like Halloween. It was dangerous, and she was perturbed that it endured year after year. Henrietta would insist on going out, she knew. Was it the ads? Something they were learning at school? Aline couldn't understand why kids liked Halloween. (She'd forgotten that she liked it herself when she was young.)

The next mail item was from the city. It read:

"DEAR HOMEOWNER,"
YOUR HOUSEHOLD HAS BECOME NONCOMPLIANT WITH THE MINIMUM STREETSIDE OFFSET ALLOWANCE (MSOA) SUBSEQUENT TO AN EMINENT DOMAIN APPROPRIATION BY THE CITY. NONCOMPLIANT STRUCTURES ARE DEMOLISHED IN ACCORDANCE TO THE DEMOLITION AND RESTRUCTURE ACT (DRA). MITIGATION FEES ARE EQUIVALENT MARKET VALUE (EMV) PLUS EXPENSES. THE EMV OF YOUR DRA AWARD IS:
$1,000,000

THE DATE OF IMPLEMENTATION OF THE REQUIREMENTS OF THE DRA PURSUANT TO BRINGING THE STRUCTURE(S) ON THIS PROPERTY INTO COMPLIANCE WITH THE MSOA IS:
OCTOBER 30

AND THE PROPERTY HAS BEEN SCHEDULED FOR DEMOLITION ON:
OCTOBER 31

PLEASE MAKE NECESSARY ARRANGEMENTS, AND RELOCATE OR LIQUIDATE PERSONAL POSSESSIONS IN ADVANCE OF THE FORMER DATE.

SIGNED,
THE DEPARTMENT OF INSTA-STRUCTURE AND HOUSING AFFAIRS (DIHA)
ADDITION DISTRICT 002

The letter didn't make much sense to Aline. Minimum street-side offset? Eminent domain appropriation? Her eyes fell again on the figure in the middle of the screen:

$1,000,000

Aline and Tom had tried to sell the place several times. It was the topic of many of their fights. For Aline, living in her rickety childhood home was a chronic aggravation, and she felt sure it was the cause of Henrietta's House Sickness. But it was valued at $900,000, and the cheapest new houses were a million dollars.

This letter changed everything. The city would pay them more to tear down the crumbling place than they could have gotten from a buyer.

Tom entered the living room with his work clothes on, his cereal bowl in one hand, chewing. Aline gestured to the screen, and he peered at it over her shoulder. She watched his eyes.

"Can you believe it?" she said.

Tom took a bite of cereal. "Barely," he said, as he chewed. "They don't give us a ton of time. Is today September 30th?"

"A month," said Aline.

"We'll have to talk more about it," said Tom, "but it seems like good news."

"It seems like great news," said Aline.

They were silent then, and both of them had the same secret thought: they imagined, for a moment, moving out on their own. Not being together anymore. If they split the money, they could each get a nice condominium.

Tom was running a little late, and he walked into the master bedroom and grabbed his coat, noticing as he did that Henrietta's BedCam seemed to be working again. He approached the viewing screen. It showed Henrietta's empty, rumpled bed.

"Finally," he muttered, not giving the matter further thought. He certainly did not speculate about whether the departure of a wild housecat from the attic had anything to do with it. Back in Henrietta's room, the counting program on her computer switched from 36,565 to 36,566.

●•· ·•●

Outside Tom was surprised to see the empty, silent street. Several blocks had been closed off, and he concluded that some road work would occur later. He entered his car, a compact red two-door, started the engine, and backed onto the vacant asphalt.

"HELLO, AND THANK YOU FOR DRIVING," said the onboard computer.

"Work," said Tom.

"TURN LEFT," said the car. "WOULD YOU LIKE TO HEAR SOME ADVERTISEMENTS FOR PRODUCTS THAT MAY INTEREST YOU WHILE YOU DRIVE?"

"Yes," said Tom, and then, "sixty percent volume, double speed. Dial work, full volume, priority."

"THANK YOU FOR USING THE ADVANCED FEATURES," said the car. A stream of advertisements issued from the car's speakers, sped up and smashed together, at sixty percent of normal volume. It formed a linguistic wallpaper against which Tom's phone dialed his work.

HAS SOMEONE YOU HAVE KNOWN DIED RECENTLY? WITH PERFUME CREMATION, ASHES ARE TRANSFORMED INTO PERFUME—THE SCENT OF LOVE. IF YOU ARE PLAGUED BY RATS TRY RAT-B-GON! RATS EAT IT, DIE, AND BECOME PENCIL ERASERS. WERE YOU RECENTLY FINISHED FROM SCHOOL? WONDERING WHAT'S NEXT? ATTEND THE GARBAGE ELIMINATION INSTITUTE—WHEN SCHOOL ENDS, THIS BEGINS.

"Hello, Tom," said a voice exactly forty percent louder than the advertisements.

"Elton," said Tom. "What's the Intermediary Technology Report?"

"Are you inbound?"

"I'll be there in—" Tom stopped to allow the car's computer to answer for him. The computer monitored his conversations and automatically filled in information that seemed appropriate. "THIRTY-THREE MINUTES."

"The report is rendering in the System Manager now."

"Stats?" said Tom.

"They're—" said Elton, and he paused to allow his own auto-complete program to fill in:

"INTEROPERABILITY 75 PERCENT, SCALABILITY 78 PERCENT, PREDICTED POTENTIAL SATURATION 35 PERCENT, MODULAR COMPONENT CROSS-MARKET INDEX 7.5, EARLY ADOPTION INDEX 5.7, PERCEIVED OBSOLESCENCE VELOCITY 85 PERCENT."

"TURN RIGHT," said the car. Tom turned right.

—CONSIDER BUYING A RING FOR THAT SPECIAL SOMEONE! THE CHERISHMENT RING IS MADE OF SPECIAL PLASTIC—PLASTIC, LIKE LOVE, LASTS FOREVER. SEASIDE HOSPITAL'S TEAM OF SURGICAL PRACTITIONERS CAN HELP YOU LOOK VIRTUALLY YOUNGER! I NEVER THOUGHT I WOULD BE OUT OF MONEY, BUT FOR THE PRICE OF ONE PAYCHECK I GOT AN ADVANCE FROM GAME OVER PAYDAY LOANS. BEEFCRAFT: LOOKS LIKE BEEF, TASTES LIKE—

"Those ratings sound good," said Tom.

"Potential saturation is a little low," said Elton.

"It doesn't matter. When the render reaches upgrade potential, we should see high numbers. Anything else?" said Tom, as if it were Elton who had called him, and not he who had called Elton.

"The DBAs have been troubleshooting inflated valuations in the System Manager. It's not a huge deal, but you may want to interface with the Virtual Operator when you get here."

"Inflated valuations?" said Tom.

"So far it's in accounts payable and interest."

"Oh, *well*," said Tom, laughing—if customers were footing the bill for a mistake, that wasn't so bad.

"TURN RIGHT," said the car. Tom turned right, merging with the flow of traffic on a cross street, which angered someone behind him, and they honked.

"BUY THE NEW SKIPPING-STONE PHONE FROM TINCAN TELE-COMM!" said the ad. Tom honked back, and his horn also said, "BUY THE NEW SKIPPING-STONE PHONE FROM TINCAN TELECOMM!"

"See you shortly, Elton," said Tom, and disconnected.

—FOR THE MAN IN CHARGE, PROFORMA PANTS SHOW EVERYONE YOU APPRECIATE THE GOOD THINGS IN LIFE. PARENTS, WHEN THE KIDS ARE GROWN, MOVE TO ADDEDGE AND ENJOY A VIEW OF THE OPEN OCEAN, BREEZES, AND THE LEISURE THAT EVERY PARENT DESERVES—

"Computer," said Tom. "Purchase two pairs ProForma pants, color gray, waist thirty-four, inseam thirty-three. Also, solicit information from AddEdge—buy-in price, resalability, location."

AUTODEDUCTION OF FOUR HUNDRED THIRTY-THREE DOLLARS FOR TWO PAIRS OF PROFORMA PANTS. INFORMATION ON ADDEDGE REQUESTED. THANK YOU FOR USING AUTODEDUCT. YOUR CONVENIENCE IS OUR REWARD.

"Computer," he said, "send information about the Garbage Elimination Institute to the following phones: me, Aline Gad-Fly, and Henrietta Gad-Fly."

"DISTRIBUTED. MERGE ONTO THE HIGHWAY." Tom merged.

"BUY THE NEW SKIPPING-STONE PHONE FROM TINCAN TELE-COMM!" honked someone behind him. Tom smiled and slowed down a little, to get them to honk again.

•• • ••

When he reached work, things were not in the same good state they'd been in minutes before. As he exited his car in the underground parking lot, his cell rang, and he saw Elton standing a hundred feet away next to the elevators, a tall, skinny man about Tom's age with short brown hair, wearing blue jeans and a T-shirt with an artificially faded slogan on it. Elton was holding his own phone to his ear. Tom answered. "Elton," he said.

"Tom, we have a situation. I need you to interface with the Virtual Operator ASAP."

"The accounts receivable glitch?" said Tom.

"It's spreading."

Tom approached Elton as they spoke, and they stepped into the elevator together. Though they were right next to each other, they continued to communicate via their phones, because the sound quality was better than face-to-face.

"Floor sixty," said Elton. A subtle lurch followed as the room rocketed skyward.

"What's the DBA report?"

"Not a storage issue—it's in the Intelligence. Anyway, the system is adding only."

"*Adding only?*" said Tom, speaking into his phone and looking blankly at Elton.

"Right—no subtraction."

The elevator doors opened, and Tom and Elton strode into a high-ceilinged hallway with one full glass wall that looked out over the Addition. From here, above the surrounding buildings, one could see the haze of pollution that covered everything in a yellow-grey cloud, through which poked some of the taller buildings, like this one.

Tom and Elton had no time to enjoy the view. They passed through a pair of automatic doors into a conference room containing a large table surrounded by twenty beige swivel-chairs.

On the wall hung a large screen, and on the screen was a face—the Virtual Operator of the System Manager. Tom had never liked the image, which had been designed before he worked at the company. The face had scarcely any nose or chin, and featured a pale haze of thin hair and light yellow eyes. The face flickered occasionally, a glitch that no one ever seemed to be able to fix. The Virtual Operator was the graphical interface for the System Manager, a program that interacted with the Intelligence Kernal, which directed all General Subsidiary Applications. Tom, though he could recite this, didn't fully understand what it meant, and this was one reason he never adequately explained his job to his daughter: he couldn't explain it to himself.

"GOOD MORNING TOM," said the Operator. When it spoke, its mouth hung open and the words emerged scratchily from the speakers at the side of the screen.

"There's a glitch in the Intelligence," said Tom. "Diagnose and repair."

"DIAGNOSING." The Operator's face flickered out of sight for a moment, and then returned. "THE GLITCH YOU REFER TO IS A GRADUATED ADJUSTMENT ALGORITHM, CURRENTLY ENGAGED TO COUNTER MALICIOUS SYSTEM CONTENT REMOVAL."

"Malicious removal?" said Tom. "What's the nature of the attack?"

The Operator looked at Tom with an expression he'd never seen it make before. It appeared…confused. "TOM," it said, "WHERE DO HENRIETTA AND HER FRIENDS GO AFTER SCHOOL?"

Smashed Sidewalks

While Henrietta, at school, wrote compositions and figured math problems, and while Aline, at home, generated accounting statistics for her clients, and while Tom, at work, tried to repair the glitch in the Intelligence Kernal, developments continued on the empty street outside their house.

More yellow vehicles arrived, in various shapes and sizes. Some looked like crustaceans, others like giraffes. Some carried massive rollers, others massive lungs. They lined up one after another and revved their engines.

The spectacle that followed was as precise as a parade. Each machine moved over the street in succession, performing the task for which it was designed. First, a massive caterpillar with jackhammer legs hammered the street into shards, and then the shards were sucked up by an enormous vacuum cleaner. Underneath the shards, a narrow old road of red bricks was revealed, which shone in the yellow autumn light just as Henrietta, Gary, and Rose had often seen through the attic windows.

The next row of vehicles used gigantic knife attachments to slice away the edge of the present street and widen it by removing the sidewalks, as well as some of the front yard of every house.

What was the purpose of all of this? The city had recently concluded, through an extensive systemwide analysis, that busy roads operate at higher efficiency if sidewalks and lawns (which scarcely anyone ever used anyway) were turned into lanes. There was one problem with this plan, however: Henrietta's house.

Henrietta's house had no front lawn. Aside from two rows of flowers and the sidewalk, it already abutted the street. The machines did what they could, lapping up the sidewalk and the flowers and leaving Henrietta's front door opening right onto what would shortly be a lane of traffic.

Next, massive dump trucks spilled mounds of hot asphalt over the bricks, up and down the block. Then a paver built to the exact width of the new street lowered its enormous roller and squashed the mounds into a steaming black plain, and a sprinkler at the rear sprayed atomized chemicals that instantly set the new surface, releasing a tremendous flowery stench. Lastly, a paint truck rolled through, squirting streams of quick-drying yellow paint—some solid lines, some dotted, some double—that defined the lanes.

Once upon a time this block had been a sleepy brick boulevard bordered on both sides by maple trees. Then it grew to a busy four-lane road with sidewalks and no trees. Now it was a six-lane highway.

Workers ascended the utility poles along the street and added the appropriate traffic signals before reconnecting the electricity and turning everything back on. The crosswalk signs were all removed, as there were no more sidewalks. The entire street had become permanently DON'T WALK.

The construction vehicles retreated, and the street reopened. Traffic flooded into the new lanes, producing instantaneous gridlock.

●●··●●

If it weren't for Henrietta's house, the road could have been wider. If a map were made of the street now, it would show Henrietta's house protruding forward from the even line of identical houses until it nearly stumbled into the street. One might wonder, looking at it from that perspective, just how long it would be before Henrietta's house went the way of the sidewalks—the way of the maple trees—the way of anything that pinched the growth of the road.

The New Route

T he school day was largely uneventful. Ms. Span was mostly pleased with the results of the Competency Exam, and she indulged a relaxed morning, smiling, nodding and dispensing universal appreciations. Tomorrow, her attentions would anxiously redirect themselves toward the next Exam, but for now she was looking back from the safe side of the hurdle they'd jumped together. Even Henrietta, though reclassified, was ensconced within the glow of the class's success.

After school, while Henrietta and Gary stood in line at the turnaround waiting for the bus, Henrietta told him she was At Risk. Gary immediately suggested that they both get Finished on purpose and become a garbage-collecting team, a proposal that didn't seem too terrible—but the incalculable amount of grief Henrietta would endure from her parents kept her from seriously considering the idea. She had to pull up her grades.

"You could cheat," said Gary.

"I can't," said Henrietta, shaking her head.

"Why not?"

"I don't know. I'm just not that kind of person."

"Well, I am," said Gary. He puffed out his chest a little.

"That's one of the things I like about you, actually," said Henrietta.

Gary punched her arm, and she punched his arm, and then he punched his own arm as Rose approached.

"Henrietta and I are going to become a garbage-collecting team," said Gary.

"Can I be on it?" said Rose.

"Definitely," said Gary.

"I have something else to tell you guys," said Henrietta as the buses slowly approached the school from far up the clogged street. She launched into the story of Mister Lady's disappearance the previous evening, which she'd been wanting to tell them since it happened.

"You saw Mister Lady *reading*?" said Gary, shaking his head in disbelief. "We always joked."

"She turned the page with a claw."

"Do you think she was angry that you caught her?"

"I don't know. I was so upset already that I wasn't paying attention. Then, before I knew it, she was gone."

"She wanted to go home," said Rose. "Back to the old town."

The buses arrived, and the children boarded together and strapped themselves in. The ride was noisy as always, what with other children talking and the constant eruption of ads from outside. They sat silently.

As the bus approached Henrietta's and Gary's stop, Henrietta noticed it wasn't slowing. She craned her neck and looked out the window.

"We're missing our stop," she said. "We're—" She saw the massive new street. There were no sidewalks anymore. If the bus dropped them off, they'd be standing right in traffic.

"The road!" said Henrietta.

"What is it?" said Gary, straining to see.

The bus rolled up to Henrietta's house and opened its door at the entrance to Henrietta's driveway. From behind came the predictable litany:

"GOT FINISHED?
ATTEND THE GARBAGE ELIMINATION INSTITUTE.
WHEN SCHOOL ENDS, THIS BEGINS!"

"DINNER COOKIES ARE DINNER AND DESSERT!
TOTALLY EFFICIENT!"

"Let's go," Henrietta shouted over the din. They unbuckled themselves and disembarked, and the bus computer logged them out, messaging their whereabouts to their parents' phones. They walked up the driveway to the carport.

"Look at my front door!" said Henrietta, pointing. The door now stood right at the edge of the freshly paved road, with a plank nailed across to keep it from opening.

"How will we get in?" said Gary.

"Over here," said Henrietta, going to the side door near the rear of the house, next to the narrow strip of plastic grass that separated Henrietta's house from the neighbors behind.

Her mother opened the door and looked down at the three of them. Henrietta expected her to be unhappy. After all, their house was now inches from six roaring lanes of traffic, and Henrietta had just brought her friends over even though she was grounded. But, surprisingly, her mother looked cheerful.

"Come in!" she said to them, and they filed into the kitchen to find a paper plate on the table piled high with Dinner Cookies.

"I thought you might need some fuel for studying," said Henrietta's mother.

"Thanks," said Gary. He immediately crammed one cookie in his mouth and another in his pants pocket.

"Mom," said Henrietta, a little uncertain how to proceed in light of her mother's unexpected good mood, "I know I'm grounded, but Gary said he'd help Rose and I study."

"Study hard!" said her mother, smiling.

Henrietta hesitated a little, still perplexed.

"Go ahead, silly!" said her mother, shooing the three of them amiably toward Henrietta's room.

Trapped!

They climbed directly into the attic and began searching for Mister Lady. Despite the considerable hours they'd spent up there during the past weeks, the network of paths through the antiques behind the bookshelves were still only partly explored, even by the intrepid Rose. Some places they just couldn't get to—spaces that had been completely boxed off by walls of old furniture.

After hunting for awhile to no avail, they regrouped glumly at the couch.

"I guess she decided she'd gotten better," said Henrietta.

"That's good, right?" said Gary.

"It's just that I liked her. And I thought she liked us."

"She did like us," said Rose. "But she had things to do."

"If I was lost and injured, I'd want to get back home," said Gary.

"I wonder if she has a family," Henrietta mused. "Do you suppose that other cat we saw is her mate?"

They went over to the windows, and looked down on the old town. The street was crowded, as it usually was at this time, with warmly dressed children returning home from school, laughing and talking, some of them even walking down the middle of the empty brick street. Mister Lady was nowhere to be seen, but Henrietta saw something else, quite unexpectedly, that caught her attention.

"Look," she said. "By the stump." The stump was currently crawling with children playing a game of tag, scurrying around the edges and across the top in pursuit and flight.

"What?" said Gary.

"That kid, there." Henrietta pointed. There was one child standing at the base of the stump who didn't look quite right. Dressed in a yellow button-up shirt and yellow pants, its face was not a person's face.

"It's . . ." said Gary. He didn't need to finish the sentence. Clearly, none of the other children could see it. As they ran past, it occasionally reached out with one long finger and tapped their foreheads.

"It's not grown up yet," Henrietta murmured.

"It isn't flickering," said Rose. She was right—it looked strangely solid compared to what Gary and Henrietta had seen the previous day.

"Have you seen it before?" said Gary, turning to Rose.

"My whole life," said Rose. "It tries to tap me, just like out there. But those kids don't mind."

"Nobody minds but us," said Henrietta, "because we're House Sick."

"What's House Sick?" said Rose.

"Nobody knows," said Henrietta. As she spoke, though, several ideas began to come together in her mind. "Wait . . ." she said, holding up one hand. She knitted her eyebrows. "We *do* know. It's that thing. I think . . . I think it doesn't like our old houses, because it can't get in!"

"I've seen it in my house," said Rose, "but you're right. It doesn't like it. It never stays."

"Maybe it's making us sick so we'll move," said Henrietta.

"But I did move," said Gary. "My mom and I left our old house, so why would it attack me on the bus?"

"Because you've been up here in the attic," said Henrietta. She clenched her hands, feeling like she'd finally grabbed something that had been hovering just beyond her reach. "On the bus it asked us where we went. And then during the Competency Exam, that was the composition question."

"That was the *Exam question*?" said Gary, aghast. He still needed to take the makeup test. "My mom said it was 'Why is it dangerous to swim?'"

Henrietta smiled despite herself—it would have been funny, in an awful way, to see Gary's careful cheating method go awry. "It can go almost anywhere—even into computers," she said. "But not into old houses. Not up here."

"But *why*?" said Gary, still not satisfied.

Their conversation ended abruptly, however, when something surprising transpired down below. The strange child stopped tapping kids on the forehead. It stepped away from the edge of the giant stump, and looked up—right at Henrietta's house. Right at the three of them looking down.

They stumbled back from the window. "It saw us!" said Gary.

Cautiously, they crawled forward and peeked over the sill. It was still looking, its yellow eyes locked on them. They fled back to the couch.

"But nobody out there *ever* sees us!" said Gary.

"If that version of it knows . . . " said Henrietta, reluctant to finish the sentence. Filled with trepidation, they approached the trapdoor, and Henrietta cautiously opened it.

There was the chair sitting atop the desk, and the desk on the tan carpet, as always. There was the bedside table, and Henrietta's canary night-light, and the windows with the shades pulled. There was the bed.

And standing next to the bed, feet together, arms at its side, was the creature. It looked frozen, like a photo, and its empty yellow eyes stared up at the three of them. Henrietta dropped the door.

"Oh, *no*," said Gary.

"Maybe it'll leave," said Henrietta. "Let's just wait."

They returned to the couch and sat together.

"Do you think it's gone yet?" said Gary immediately. He reflexively pulled his phone from his pocket and looked at it. "Hey," he said. "It's . . . well, it's not really working, but it's kind of working." He showed them the screen, which was lit, and the digital numbers that indicated the time were there, but crawling at a fraction of their normal pace. "Uh oh," he said, and they all simultaneously reached the same conclusion: When you're up in this attic, where time is frozen, it doesn't matter how long you wait. The thing down below will be there, from your perspective, forever.

"But it arrived after we climbed up," said Henrietta. "It came later. So time must be passing a little, or just passing for it, or . . ."

"Let's keep waiting," said Rose.

They sat for another few moments in silence. "We should try to distract ourselves," said Henrietta. Gary picked up an old deck of cards he'd found some weeks ago, and started laying them out with Rose for Solitaire, a game they'd learned from one of the dusty attic books.

Henrietta picked up *Early Town* from the coffee table. It was still open to the page Mister Lady had been reading, which was an odd-looking, close-up map that showed Boardwalk, the street right outside Henrietta's house. It appeared to be two maps, one laid on top of the other. The bottom map was the one Henrietta had seen before, of the single-lane brick boulevard. The other map, printed on transparent paper and laid atop the first, showed the road Henrietta had grown up with—four lanes with sidewalks.

Henrietta tried to puzzle the pieces together. Was this a map of the future— or what *was* the future, once upon a time?

"Hey," she said to Gary and Rose, but the moment she spoke, a loud *bang!* sounded from outside. The children started and looked at the windows.

Their view of the enormous trees was obscured by a young man standing outside atop a ladder. He wore a red checked shirt and a blue cotton cap. In one hand he held a hammer, and in the other a two-by-four plank. He looked in but didn't appear to see the children.

"Who is that?" said Gary.

"I don't know . . ." said Henrietta. Then she did know. "It's Al! My grandfather!" But it wasn't the Al she knew. It was Al as he had once been, decades before Henrietta was born—a young man. He lifted the plank and began nailing it to the outside of the house, across the windows.

"What's he doing?" said Gary.

"He's making the house like it is now," said Henrietta.

"We've got to stop him!" said Gary.

"We can't," said Henrietta. "He has to do it. The city's about to knock down the trees and turn the road into more traffic lanes. Look." She held up *Early Town* so Gary and Rose could see the overlaid maps.

"But that just happened!" said Gary.

"It just happened *again*, you mean. It happened the first time then, and again now," said Henrietta.

"The same thing all over," said Gary.

"Do you think Mister Lady left the book open there on purpose?" said Rose.

Outside, Al nailed another board on the window, blocking out more light. The attic began to darken.

"Why's he doing that?" said Gary.

"So the trees don't shatter the windows when they fall," said Henrietta.

Al disappeared down the ladder for a moment and then returned with more boards. The light diminished further, the shadows deepened, and soon Al's face was no longer visible. The last board was in place, leaving the attic in pitch darkness. They listened to the final strokes of the hammer. Then, silence.

"You guys," said Gary's voice, strained and a little high-pitched. Henrietta could imagine his eyebrows bunching together.

"What is it?" said Henrietta.

"I'm afraid of the dark. Could we open the trapdoor again, just for a second?" There was a cold tremor in his voice, and Henrietta recognized that he was starting to panic. She recalled his disastrous descent the first time she'd shown him the place.

"Let's all go together," said Henrietta. She took Gary's and Rose's hands, and they shuffled through the darkness to the trapdoor.

Henrietta pulled it open a crack. The light from the bedroom flooded in, and Gary began a relieved sigh that caught almost immediately in his throat as he looked down. The thing was still waiting below, fixing them with its steady stare. Henrietta slowly closed the door again.

"You know," Henrietta said, "I remember seeing some candles on one of the bookshelves, once. Did you guys see those?"

"Yeah," said Gary. "And a box next to them—matches!"

"Remember when we watched a movie about them in class?" said Henrietta. "*Don't Strike Those Matches*. A kid burns his house down."

"That movie was really good," breathed Gary.

"You two stay here," said Henrietta. "I'm going to find them." She released her friends' hands and felt her way across the floor. She maneuvered behind the coffee table to the base of the nearest bookshelf and slid her hands up the spines of the old books until she reached the top shelf, letting her fingers skim the outlines of the items there. A bronze baby shoe. A glass ashtray. A bookend. And . . . a candelabra, loaded with seven long tapers. She curled her fingers around the metal base. With her other hand, she continued searching until she found the small cardboard box.

She crawled back to the coffee table, set the candelabra on it, and opened the box. Inside it felt like a bunch of sticks. "Do you remember how that kid lit them in the movie?" she said.

"There should be some red stuff on one end," said Gary, "and you swipe it against the side."

"I can't see anything," said Henrietta.

"The bigger end," said Rose, who dealt with matches frequently in the Library.

She felt inside the box. Each stick had a little bulb on one end. She swiped one against the side of the box. "It didn't work."

"Feel around on the box," said Gary. "One side should have a rough strip. I have a couple in my trash collection, and I think they're all the same."

He was right. Henrietta tried again, and—*Fiss!* The match ignited. She held it to the wick of one of the long candles, which caught easily and glowed with a steady, swelling light. She lit two more candles, and then dropped the match on the floor and stomped it out thoroughly.

"You did it!" said Gary. It was comforting to have a little light, even if their situation was the same as before.

"What now?" said Gary.

"Keep waiting, I guess," said Henrietta.

"We should sleep soon," said Rose

Gary rubbed his eyes. "Yeah," he said. "I'm almost as tired as I am scared."

"It does seem pretty late," said Henrietta.

"We could camp up here," said Gary, and for the first time in a while there was a hopeful note in his voice. He'd always wanted to camp.

"There are probably blankets somewhere," said Henrietta.

"In the dresser," said Rose. Henrietta handed her the candelabra, and Rose led the way back behind the bookcases to an old wooden dresser. Henrietta pulled open the top drawer to reveal a pile of neatly folded blankets. She and Gary scooped up several of them, and they all returned to the main room, where they made up three little beds on the floor next to the couch.

"I don't think I've ever gone to sleep without brushing my teeth," said Henrietta. "I hope they don't rot."

"They won't," said Gary. "I've done it."

"Doesn't your mom make you?"

"Sometimes I fake it." He opened his mouth wide, showing two rows of reasonably clean-looking teeth in the candlelight.

"When I first found Mister Lady up here, I told my mom I was using the bathroom, but I was really getting some bandages," said Henrietta. The two of them grinned at one another, pleased about their shared history of mischievousness.

"I've lied, too," said Rose. "To everyone. About everything." And then, finally, she told the story she had been forbidden to tell.

She told it because she trusted her two friends and because they had trusted her, been kind to her, and helped her. She began with her home, the Library, with its thousands of old books stretching to high ceilings. She told them about the Subscribers who arrived in the dead of night; about elaborate secret knocks; and about thieves who read historical romances, dumpster diving scientists obsessed with narrative poetry, and former telecommunications employees who loved cookbooks. Once she got started, she kept talking until it was all out, and when she finished, Henrietta and Gary were dumbstruck.

Henrietta was first to form a question: "You have friends from the *Old City*?" she said. "What are they like? Are they scary?"

"The Subscribers are nice," said Rose. "They come over and fix books with my dad."

"How do they live?" said Gary. "Do they kidnap people?"

"They find things," said Rose. "Like in trash cans."

"They *steal trash?*" said Gary, his eyes widening.

"Sometimes it isn't really trash," said Rose. "All of my clothes I'm wearing. My shoes."

Henrietta and Gary looked at Rose's shoes. In the low light of the candles, they looked like regular shoes, white plastic with Velcro straps.

"Those were in a dumpster?" said Gary. He reached out and touched them gingerly.

"Someone outgrew them," said Rose.

"This is amazing," said Gary. "Amazing." Everything he'd ever thought about the world was turned on its head in an instant. Trash wasn't trash. Criminals weren't criminals. He frowned, and then smiled, and then bit his lip.

"Why didn't you tell us this before?" said Henrietta.

"My parents said if I ever told we'd have to leave the Library, and I'd have to quit school."

"*I* won't tell," said Gary. "Not a soul. Not ever. Unless it's by accident," he corrected. "Sometimes I say things by accident."

"I'll remind you not to," said Henrietta. She turned back to Rose. "But how do your parents keep the whole thing secret? And why is an old library sitting out in the middle of the Addition?"

"I don't know," said Rose to both questions.

"I can hardly believe it," said Henrietta. She stared at Rose as if looking at a complete stranger. This little kid was a never ending font of surprises, and

Henrietta felt proud to have her as a friend.

Gary said, "My only secret is that I can't read."

"But you can read now," said Rose.

"That's true." Gary grinned. "I guess I don't have any secrets."

"You cheat on tests and collect garbage," said Henrietta, and she leaned over and blew out the candles. In the darkness, they crawled under the covers they'd laid out, and rested their heads on the couch cushions.

After talking with his friends, Gary felt a little less scared to be in the dark, and he drifted off quickly. Henrietta and Rose followed soon after, both exhausted and scared, but, for the moment, safe.

A Death in the Family

After the children departed to Henrietta's room to study, Aline returned to her work, but even as she prepared a lengthy accounting report, part of her mind continued to ponder the mail from the city. That money could make her life into something she'd begun to think it would never be: happy. Perhaps she could escape the feeling, one she'd had for so long, of being trapped. She wondered how Henrietta would react to the news, and realized that she had no idea at all.

Aline didn't feel very close to her daughter. As Henrietta had grown into childhood and revealed her personality, the two of them had begun to clash. Henrietta couldn't seem to do anything the normal way, and not because she lacked the ability. Rather, she seemed to intentionally avoid fitting in and doing what people required of her. Aline had wondered, on occasion, if Henrietta wasn't her real daughter. Maybe her real daughter had been switched with someone else's at the hospital, and some set of sloppy, willful, uncharming parents were wondering how they'd managed to produce a beautiful, obedient, tidy little girl.

Aline's phone rang. She looked at the screen and frowned. It was Al. For a moment, she became angry. Why would he be calling her? She'd told him in no uncertain terms when he'd married her mother that she wanted nothing to do with him. It had been the last straw, and she was still, even now, furious that her mother had—

Her heart sank as she realized why Al was calling. There was only one possible reason. She turned away from her computer and answered the call. "Mother," she whispered into the phone.

"Aline, I'm sorry," said Al's scratchy old voice. "She passed away peacefully in her sleep. This morning."

And the worst of all: Aline hadn't seen her mother since the birthday party, over a month ago. She'd been so angry, about . . . something.

"I'd like to talk to you a bit about memorial arrangements," Al said stiffly.

"I need to go," said Aline. "I'll . . ." she didn't even finish the sentence, just disconnected the call. She turned to the windows where the slow mass of traffic passed within inches of her house. The cars seemed miles away.

The Escape Plan

Henrietta's eyes opened in the pitch darkness. It took her a moment to remember where she was—the attic, with the windows blocked off, and Gary and Rose beside her.

"What was that?" said Gary's voice.

Something had awakened them both.

"I don't know," said Henrietta.

Then came a whooshing sound, like a broom scraping across a floor. It came from the blocked windows.

"It's the trees," said Henrietta. "They're getting chopped down!" The sound continued, and Henrietta imagined the grand limbs toppling, their red and gold leaves brushing the house as they fell.

"I wonder how much time has passed," said Henrietta. She sat up, felt for the box of matches and the candelabra on the table, and lit the candles.

Gary and Rose sat up in their piles of blankets. Rose's black hair was frizzed out from tossing and turning, and Gary's was a spiky thicket. They certainly looked as though they'd been asleep for a while.

They went to the trapdoor and cracked it open, although they all had a feeling about what they'd find. They were right. The creature hadn't moved. Its eyes were still fixed on the entrance.

"I'm kind of hungry," said Gary once Henrietta replaced the trapdoor.

"Me, too," said Henrietta. Her stomach growled.

"I wish we could eat cobwebs, like Mister Lady," said Gary. He plucked one from an empty bookshelf and eyed it critically.

Rose tapped the *Bestiary*'s cover, on the table. "Have you ever looked up the Wikkeling in here?" she asked. Gary and Henrietta looked at her blankly.

"The what?" said Henrietta.

"The Wikkeling. In your room," said Rose, gesturing toward the trapdoor.

"How do you—" said Gary, and then stopped himself. "Never mind," he said. "You just know everything. I accept that."

They sat at the coffee table, and Gary and Rose looked on as Henrietta flipped to the table of contents and skimmed it fruitlessly. She went to the index. Nothing. Page by page, they examined all the pictures.

"I guess they didn't know about it," she said as she turned past "Alphabeetle," "False Apple," and "Tree Goat." Then a thought occurred. "You know what, though. My grandfather's version might be better. It's a later edition."

"I wish our phones worked," said Gary.

Henrietta continued flipping through the ancient book a page at a time, until she landed on the very first thing she'd ever looked up: *Housecats—Wild*. She remembered sitting with Mister Lady, studying the strange words, combing the mildewy attic dictionary for the meanings of terms like *ingress* and *egress*. She contemplated those terms now, still locked in their same sentence.

. . . many homes contain so-called "Cat Halls," thought to encourage Ingress and Egress.

"Hey," she said, putting her finger on the sentence.

"What is it?" said Gary.

"Cat Halls," said Henrietta. "Ingress and egress!"

"You're right!" said Rose.

"What? What?" said Gary, looking from one of them to the other. "What are they?"

Henrietta grabbed the candelabra.

"Coming and going," said Rose.

"People used to put doors in their attics for wild housecats," said Henrietta. "That's how Mister Lady got in here, and it's how we're going to get out."

The Cat Hall

They split up, each taking a candle and moving behind the bookshelves into the various deep corners of the attic. Now that they had an idea to work toward, the attic seemed a little less scary. As she headed down a dark aisle bordered by stacks of old paintings of the ocean, Henrietta heard Gary and Rose rooting around elsewhere, moving boxes, squeezing between stacked chairs. Suddenly, she found herself smiling. They were going to figure this out!

She balanced her candle on a tabletop and started moving some of the paintings to see if the hall might be hidden there when a shout stopped her, echoing through the attic.

"*I found it!*"

Henrietta and Gary followed Rose's triumphant exclamation along a row of ceramic plant containers sitting on narrow plant stands and wooden magazine racks until they reached a large stack of luggage.

Rose's voice seemed to emerge from under the pile. Henrietta held out her candle and saw a narrow, dark space framed by an alligator-skin purse, a wooden hatbox, and a denim-sided briefcase.

"Are you *under*?" said Henrietta.

"It goes through," said Rose's muted voice.

Henrietta and Gary knelt and squirmed one after the other into the luggage tunnel. Henrietta held her candle carefully, remembering the part in *Don't Strike Those Matches* when a flame ignited a boy's hair. The tunnel ran for about fifteen feet, and they emerged in a little room formed of the backs of several bookshelves and one wall of the attic. Rose jumped up and down in triumph when they arrived, pointing toward her find.

The cat hall was right there, at the intersection between wall and floor, a miniature doorway just large enough for a wild housecat to squeeze through—or a kid. Its frame was carved with intricate designs, and a message had been engraved over the lintel. Gary leaned down to read it.

EAT OUR COBWEBS, CHASE OUR RATS. IN THIS HOUSE WE LOVE OUR CATS.

Henrietta peered through the cat hall. "It's dark outside. Time must be passing out there—it looks like the middle of the night."

"I don't get it," said Gary.

"It's unpredictable," said Rose.

Henrietta knelt and stuck her head through the cat hall. Below lay the narrow lane of plastic turf that ran between the back of her house and the back of the neighbors'. Neither house had any windows on this side—it was an unused area. Henrietta felt dizzy as she contemplated the drop. She pulled her head back in. "It's really far," she said.

"It's not too bad," said Rose. "We just need a landing pad."

Before Henrietta could formulate a follow-up question, Rose took her candle and crawled back out through the luggage, into the attic proper. Henrietta and Gary looked at one another, and Gary shrugged. Rose soon returned, dragging the blankets and pillows they'd slept on.

"Landing pad," she said again, and pushed the blankets through the cat hall, letting them fall to the ground outside. She stuck her head through and looked down. "We'll need a lot more."

They all went into the attic and located as many soft objects as they could find—bedding and ornamental pillows, towels, a few old teddy bears, two bath mats, seven throw rugs, pants, shirts, a fluffy down parka. . . . Henrietta quickly lost track of it all as they dropped one item after another onto the growing pad below.

"Good enough," Rose declared finally, peering down through the cat hall at the prodigious pile. She pulled her head back in and stood. "Gary, you first."

"M-me?" said Gary.

"You're tough, but sometimes you don't realize it," said Rose. Gary opened his mouth to make a retort, but closed it again. He blinked several times, realizing that Rose was correct. In fact, her assessment was one of the truest things anyone had ever said about him. With a thoughtful, determined frown, he blew out his candle and set it aside. He lay on his belly and entered the cat hall feet first. He began wiggling through. "It's chilly outside!" he said as he progressively disappeared. "Okay, this is as far as I can go, so . . . I'm going to drop. Wish me luck!"

"Good lu—" said Henrietta, and Gary was gone. Henrietta and Rose scrambled forward and looked out after him. He was lying on the landing pad. For

a moment, he was still, and then he rolled onto the ground, got up, and showily dusted himself off. "I'm okay!" he called up. "It was . . . fun! You next, Henrietta!"

Henrietta blew out her candle. "Rose, do you think I can make it?"

"Definitely," said Rose.

Henrietta put her feet out, and squirmed through the hall, feeling the cool night air on her ankles. Soon, she'd gone as far as she could. She'd have to drop.

"Wish me luck," she said.

"Good luck," said Rose, and she wiggled her fingers to indicate the luck flying out.

With a sick feeling in her stomach, Henrietta let go, and she saw, in a blur, the attic disappear, the door shrink away, and the siding of the house flying past along with cold air and dizziness. . . .

Foomp!

She hit the pile, sinking deep down and then rolling off.

Gary hovered over her.

"Are you okay?" he said.

Henrietta stood and took a couple of shaky steps. She looked up at the house, and saw, far above, the cat hall, and Rose's face looking down through it. She smiled. She waved up to Rose. "It *was* kind of fun!" she said.

The yellow glow of Rose's candle went out. Then her feet appeared through the door. Soon, she was as far as she could go, and she dropped. The speed of the plummet was a little stomach-churning, but Rose sank into the soft pile and emerged quickly, bouncing right onto her feet.

All three of them laughed from nervousness and relief as they looked up at the cat hall far above.

"What now?" said Rose.

"Call my grandfather," said Henrietta, taking out her phone. She looked at the screen, about to search for Al's listing, but she froze.

"What is it?" said Gary.

Wordlessly, Henrietta turned the phone around and showed it.

WHERE DO YOU GO?

She placed it on the ground and stepped on it firmly, crushing it. Gary perused his own phone for a moment, frowned, put it next to Henrietta's, and smashed it, too.

"We've got to get out of here," said Henrietta. "We should try to get to my grandfather's."

"How?" said Gary.

"I don't know. It's called Sunset Estates. I know the address."

"Maybe we can use my phone," said Rose.

"Your phone?" said Henrietta. "I thought—"

"I lied," said Rose. She reached into her pocket and pulled out her phone. Gary raised his eyebrows when he saw it. It was last year's model and looked a bit ridiculous. Instead of the curvy oval shape of this year's phones it was rectangular, with sharp corners.

Rose opened it and held it out so Henrietta and Gary could see the screen. It was blank except for a blinking green cursor.

"It's broken," said Gary.

"It isn't," said Rose. "It's cracked."

"Cracked?" said Gary.

"My mom cracked it. It's off the system."

"I don't understand," said Henrietta.

"You said the Wikkeling was in the school computer," said Rose. "Now it's on your phones. But mine is manual." She started typing numbers onto her screen.

"What are you doing?" said Henrietta.

"Calling some friends."

"You . . . you just *know* the number?" said Henrietta.

"I memorized it," said Rose. She finished typing. She held the phone to her ear and stepped away as she began a whispered conversation.

A moment later, she pocketed the phone and turned to Henrietta and Gary. "They're coming," she said.

"Who?" said Gary.

"Friends from the Old City," said Rose.

A chill ran through Henrietta's spine as she heard the words. She wondered if Rose's "friends" would make things better or worse.

All three children jumped nearly out of their skins as a voice sounded from behind the landing pad they'd assembled.

"WHERE DO YOU GO?" it said.

Frightening Friends

The Wikkeling had appeared from around the front corner of the house. "WHERE DO YOU GO?" it asked again, repeating the words exactly, the scratchy echo resounding down its pink throat as its mouth hung slack. Its body flickered out of sight for a moment, and when it returned it was a step closer.

"You want to know where we were?" said Henrietta, hoping to perhaps reason with it. "We were in the attic. Up there." She pointed toward the cat hall. The Wikkeling looked up.

"Why does it matter?" said Henrietta. "Why don't you leave us alone?"

The Wikkeling flicked off and on again, returning to sight with one hand raised, its long, waxen index finger pointed at them.

Then another voice sounded, from behind the children at the opposite corner of the house. "Rose!" it lisped. Gary clutched his heart reflexively, wondering if he could possibly be any more nervous that he already was.

The children turned to see two strangers, and to Henrietta and Gary they looked more terrifying even than the Wikkeling. The one who'd spoken was wiry and bald with a pale face and a streaked gray beard. He wore a black long-sleeved shirt, grimy gray pants, and a pair of dark green knee-high rubber boots. His pants were held up with suspenders that appeared to be laminated strips cut from plastic grocery bags.

The second man was equally dirty, and a mountain—at least six and a half feet tall. His dark red hair was wrapped into a loose bun, and his face was scruffy with stubble. A streak of grease was smudged across his forehead, as if he'd scratched an itch with a dirty hand.

Rose leaped forward and threw herself into the arms of the bald man. "That was fast!" she said. "We need help. We're going to Sunset Estates. We're in danger." She pointed at the Wikkeling, which had stopped its advance for a moment, perhaps to assess the developing situation. It was immediately apparent that the two visitors couldn't see it, however, and Rose continued, "We need to go *now*." Her voice filled with a tremendous authority that made her seem much older.

The bald man shrugged. "Jump on, then," he said, kneeling. Rose scrambled onto his back, putting her arms around his neck, and he stood.

The enormous man knelt also, and indicated that Henrietta and Gary should follow Rose's example. "Nice to meet you," he said in a scratchy voice. "My name is Oak."

Henrietta hesitated.

"Hurry," said Rose from her perch atop the bald man. Henrietta and Gary both pulled themselves onto Oak's impossibly broad back. Henrietta grabbed his left shoulder, and Gary his right.

The two strangers began to run, and Oak's gait almost shook Henrietta from her purchase. She grabbed tighter, curling her hands into his thick clothing as she looked ahead, wondering where they could possibly go. The only option she knew of was the sidewalk—and that was gone now. But if you're the kind of person who can't be seen on sidewalks without getting arrested, you learn other ways. Henrietta had never noticed, for instance, that the rear alley behind her house also ran behind the house next door, and the one after that, continuing all the way up the block if you knew how to follow it: a little to the left, between two fences, and behind a narrow shed.

Henrietta and Gary held on for dear life against the jolts of Oak's long strides. She glanced back briefly—the Wikkeling was already out of sight behind them. She breathed a sigh of relief. Next to her, Gary said, "G-g-g—d-d-d," which meant, "Good riddance!" His words were pounded down to two consonants by Oak's gait.

They made another turn down a narrow, pitch-dark alley between two tall buildings. Behind them, the sounds of traffic disappeared, replaced with sounds of splashing—they were running through water. Oak's stride slowed a little, and the jouncing settled enough for Henrietta to speak.

"Where are we?" she said, still holding on tightly.

"You won't understand the route," said Oak. "We're . . . behind the scenes, you might say." Ahead of them, the bald man turned suddenly right, disappearing. Oak followed, and they emerged into a wider alley with a few streetlamps overhead. Henrietta saw that they were running over bricks.

"Bricks," she said to Gary. "Just like through the windows."

"This is incredible!" said Gary. "I can't believe I never knew about this."

"We're in the Old City now," said Oak. "School buses never go back here—there's no children." They took another turn into an open alley square at the intersection of several buildings. The bald man had stopped ahead, and Rose was climbing off. Oak knelt and let Henrietta and Gary dismount. They both looked around in wonderment at the old buildings rising into the darkness around them. "Wow, wow," Gary muttered under his breath as he took it all in.

"Rosie, you better explain yourself," the bald man lisped, a little out of breath. "I'm of a mind to call your parents. The whole gosh-dang Old City is looking for you right now. And *these two*," he gestured toward Henrietta and Gary. "The whole gosh-dang Addition is looking for them. And blaming us, I might add." He snorted. Then he nodded at Henrietta and Gary. "Nice to meet you both, by the way," he said, loping forward and extending his hand. "The name's OK."

"OK?" said Henrietta.

"All right," said OK. He smiled, and Henrietta saw he was missing his front teeth, which explained his lisp. "Now go ahead, Rose, with that explanation."

"We can see an invisible creature," said Rose. "It's called the Wikkeling. It's after us."

"You're *sure* this ain't a game," said OK sternly.

"I'm sure," said Rose. "We think Henrietta's grandfather can help us. He's got a *Bestiary*."

"An Alcott *Bestiary*?" said OK. Rose looked at Henrietta.

"That's right," said Henrietta. "Do you know it?"

"Saw one once," said OK. "A beautiful old book. You think your Wick-ling will be in there, do you?"

Just then a low rumbling sound entered the alleyway. "Here comes yer ride," said OK. Then he pointed to the greasy dumpster. "Jump in here, and the truck'll scoop you up with the trash." He picked up Rose, carried her to the lip, and dropped her inside. "C'mon," he said to Henrietta and Gary.

"You want us to get in *there*?" said Henrietta, spreading her fingers in revulsion.

"Wow!" said Gary. He immediately clambered over the top and flipped inside, disappearing. "Wow!" he said again, his voice echoing within.

When Henrietta didn't move, OK gestured to Oak, who scooped her up and heaved her gracelessly through the opening. "*Augh*," said Henrietta as the terrible thick smell entered her nose.

OK's face appeared above them. "Pay attention, and make sure you get off at the right stop." He grinned at Henrietta. "Pretend you're on the school bus." He disappeared, and the rumbling grew quickly until Henrietta could feel it vibrating in the trash bags all around her. The dumpster began to tilt.

"Look out!" yelled Gary as the trash shifted, tumbling over itself. Henrietta tried to keep her balance, but before she knew it she was midair.

She landed on a soft pile, and a black trash bag flopped down on her head.

Gary rushed to his feet, his eyes wide. "We're riding in a garbage truck!" he said, obviously thrilled.

"This is gross," said Henrietta, pinching her nose with one smelly hand.

"Are you kidding?" said Gary. He looked out from the open rear of the truck as it pulled from the alleyway and into traffic, the roar of the engine mixing with the sounds of other cars and trucks all around. "I've wanted to do this for my *entire life!*" He held his hands up in the air, striking a triumphant pose. "*GARBAGE TRUCK!*" he yelled.

Surrounding the truck were lanes of traffic, and the children peeked out at the cars.

"Stay down," said Rose. Henrietta tackled Gary, and they both fell into the trash. Gary was laughing hysterically.

"I can't believe you wanted to do this," said Henrietta.

"I thought *everyone* wanted to do this," said Gary.

The truck took a slow turn onto a larger road, and the children peeked out. They were in one of the middle lanes of a ten-lane thoroughfare, high enough to look down through the windshields and see the blank faces of all the people driving.

"Watch for Sunset Estates," said Rose. "If we miss it, we'll get compacted."

"Compacted?" said Henrietta.

"Squashed," said Rose, "when the truck reaches the dump."

They began looking in earnest.

FindEm™

The news of her mother's death shook Aline, wiping her daughter and her studying friends entirely from her mind. She started to get dinner ready in a daze, threw out the breakfast dishes, and worked halfheartedly on a project for one of her clients.

Tom returned late from work. He entered the kitchen holding his cell phone in front of his face, reading something on the small screen. He pocketed the phone and gave Aline an exhausted look. "How was your day?" he asked.

"My mother passed," said Aline.

Tom stopped short, caught off guard. Then he put his arms around Aline, who held him tightly.

"I knew she didn't have long, but . . . I never called. She raised me here, in this house." Aline pulled away from Tom and looked disconsolately around.

"Did you tell Henrietta?" said Tom.

"Not yet. She's studying with her friends." At that moment, Aline realized that Henrietta's room had been uncommonly quiet for a very long time. Without another word, she walked to Henrietta's closed door and entered.

Henrietta, Gary, and Rose were not there. Aline yelled, and Tom raced in from the living room. He was already on his cell, and Aline activated hers also.

She accessed FindEm™, a tracking program parents used to locate kids.

HELLO! LET US HELP YOU FINDEM™!

Aline scrolled down the Find menu, which contained herself, her mother, Tom, and Henrietta. She selected Henrietta and clicked FINDEM™.

FINDING . . .

Tom was similarly occupied. Aline sat on the edge of Henrietta's bed, holding the phone tightly in both hands. After a few moments, the word "Finding" was replaced on both their phones with

SORRY. CONTACT THE POLICE? Y/N

Aline selected *Y* and held the phone to her ear.

"Seaside Precinct. Missing persons," said a disinterested woman's voice on Aline's phone.

"Henrietta Gad-Fly," said Aline.

"Scanning for the phone," said the officer. "I don't see it active."

"What does that mean?" said Aline. "Is the battery down?"

"The phone was destroyed. When did you last see your daughter?"

"A couple of hours ago."

"Where?"

"In her bedroom, with her friends," said Aline.

"Have you searched the house to ensure she and her friends aren't hiding?"

"Well, no, but if her phone is destroyed—" She looked around as she said it.

Tom knelt and peered under Henrietta's bed.

"Sometimes children destroy phones and hide because they're angry at their parents," said the officer. "Maybe she's angry at you."

"I . . . don't think so," said Aline.

"I suggest you search the house. All I can do here is scan her cell records to see if a malfunction message was logged. What are her friends' names?"

"Gary Span, and Rose Soldottir," said Aline.

"We'll check their phones as well."

"Thank you," said Aline. She hung up.

"Why is Henrietta's chair sitting on her desk?" said Tom. There was no immediate answer to this question, and the two of them split up and searched the house. Aline opened the kitchen cupboards and moved couches away from the walls. She felt a terrible, constricting ache in her heart.

Tom went through the master bedroom and the bathroom, and everywhere else he could think of, and eventually collapsed on the living room couch. Aline sat next to him, and her phone rang. The officer informed her that Henrietta had been classified as a Person of Unknown Whereabouts, as were Gary and Rose, whose parents were also being contacted.

Tom and Aline were directed to search the house again. Had they looked in the freezer? The toilet tank? The oven?

Tom, fed up, seized the phone. "She's obviously been kidnapped!" he shouted.

Attacked

The garbage truck turned off the ten-lane arterial into a residential neighborhood.

Gary stood tall, the wind whipping his hair, a wide smile on his face. Henrietta, nauseated from the stench of the garbage, focused on scanning the buildings around her for anything familiar, and soon spotted the sign for Sunset Estates.

The truck pulled into the Estates, passed a long stretch of identical homes, and paused at a row of dumpsters.

"*Now!*" said Rose.

They extricated themselves from the trash, jumped from the stinking truck onto the asphalt drive, and beelined for the shadows at the side of the nearest town home, even as one of the garbage collectors hopped from the truck's cab.

"I wish my mom drove a garbage truck instead of a car," Gary whispered, panting a little from the sprint. "So," he said, taking in the line of identical houses. "How do we figure out which is your grandpa's?"

"His address," said Henrietta. "Zero five, zero seven, six three two."

The sidewalks running through Sunset Estates' honeycomb of streets were silent. All of the old people were inside, probably sleeping, and no one but the garbage collector was driving through. The sound of the truck's grumbling engine diminished behind them as they walked.

They figured out the pattern of addresses and headed toward Al's.

"I hope he's home," said Rose.

"I hope he's awake," said Gary.

All of the town homes followed the same architectural pattern: Garage, porch, front door. Garage, porch, front door.

"Just a few more," said Henrietta.

"WHERE DO YOU GO?" said a voice. The children all turned, eyes wide, to find the Wikkeling out in the street, pacing them. Its haunting, flickering face gaped. A sound of static pulsed from its open mouth.

"*Run*," said Henrietta.

The Wikkeling blipped along, appearing and disappearing, easily in step with them as they fled. Henrietta glanced at the address they were rushing past: Al's was next.

Garage.

Porch.

Front door. The Wikkeling closed in perilously as Henrietta pressed the doorbell, which began its cheery rendition of "Jingle Bells."

"Grandpa!" Henrietta shouted.

This time, the Wikkeling went for Rose.

Its long finger stretched out and tapped her, but instead of disappearing as usual, the Wikkeling's finger stuck to Rose's head, as if it were glued there.

Rose collapsed as the front door opened to reveal Al, an old book in one hand and a questioning look on his face as he took in the scene.

"Henrietta?" he said. "What—"

"Let us in!" said Henrietta.

"Who—" said Al.

Henrietta grabbed Rose's arm to support her. "Hurry!" she said. Gary grabbed Rose's other arm.

Al stepped aside to make way, and Henrietta and Gary stumbled in with Rose in tow. The Wikkeling, still attached to Rose by its index finger, dragged with Rose across the threshold.

The door swung closed behind them. Rose and the Wikkeling lay in a heap on the floor.

"Stop it!" Henrietta shouted.

"The *Wikkeling*?" said Al, his brow furrowing.

"You can see it?" said Gary.

"Release her!" said Al, whacking at it with the old book he held. Surprisingly, the Wikkeling recoiled as it was struck, and it swatted at the book, knocking it out of Al's hand and ripping a few pages from the binding.

"Books!" said Henrietta, grabbing Al's arm.

"What?" said Al.

"Books! Old books!" She turned to Gary. "Gary—it's not just that the houses are old. Rose's house is a library, and so is the attic! It's the books, too!"

"You're right," said Gary.

Henrietta turned to Al. "We're taking Rose into your basement."

Al asked no further questions, but knelt painfully on his old knees and picked up Rose. The Wikkeling stood, its finger still stuck to Rose's forehead, and walked along beside.

"Don't let it touch you," said Henrietta. She ran ahead and opened the basement door, ushering Gary in first. "Get the light," she said. Gary flipped the switch, and the fluorescent lights flickered on.

Henrietta descended ahead of Al, Rose, and the Wikkeling.

As Al went, the Wikkeling didn't follow—it rooted itself to the spot on the top step and its arm began to stretch, unwinding from its body like a garden hose.

Once Al and Rose reached the bottom, the Wikkeling's finger disengaged with a *pop* and its arm recoiled up the stairs. It moaned out a sound like twisting metal, and flickered out for a moment. When it reappeared a second later, it was sitting on the top step, holding its hands to its head.

Al laid Rose on the basement couch, and the three gathered around her.

"Is she breathing?" said Henrietta as Gary knelt and listened.

"Yes," he said.

Henrietta glanced up the stairwell at the Wikkeling. "Look at it," she said. It sat there, head in its hands, as if in pain.

"Tell me what's going on," said Al.

"We need to see your *Bestiary*," said Henrietta.

Al ducked into one of the rows of bookshelves and brought out the copy he'd shown Henrietta on her previous visit.

"Is there an entry on the Wikkeling?" said Henrietta. "You knew its name when you saw it."

"When I was young," said Al, "I used to see it. Everybody did."

"Just . . . walking around?"

"There was a story that it was supposed to protect people. But it disappeared as time went on. I'd started to think it was a dream."

"We're trapped again," said Gary, looking up the stairs where the Wikkeling was still seated miserably on the top step, between them and the exit.

"It has never protected us from anything," said Henrietta.

Al flipped to the index of the *Bestiary*.

"Here it is," he said. "Under *Nonliving Creatures*."

```
Wikkeling, The:
It is argued in recent years whether the Wikkeling exists or is
simply a story, though this author is compelled to assert his
conviction that this unique creature is real, and was once seen
by many. As time has gone on, and sightings have diminished, its
existence has become increasingly mythologized.
    The Wikkeling was engineered by two scientists named Henrift
and Andi in the early days of civilization to destroy the
Draageling (page 345) and to generally harness the power of
nature toward human industry. It served faithfully in the outset,
but grew maleficent, even killing its creators. The Wikkeling
became increasingly reclusive as years wore on, shrinking from
sight until finally absenting itself altogether from human
contact. Its whereabouts are no longer known. Of those who
believe in its existence, some maintain that it moved away, some
that it died, and some that it remains invisibly among humans.
    It is said to be violently repelled by highly time-resistant
objects such as old books, old trees, and wild housecats (whose
shrinking population is sometimes attributed to the Wikkeling).
    —Observed by H.G-F. Recorded by A.A.
```

Henrietta was thinking hard. "Al," she said, "remember the cat I told you about?"

"Yes."

"She got better, and finally left. I wonder—if the Wikkeling doesn't like wild housecats, is there any way. . . ."

"Right," said Al, and he turned and disappeared again into one of the long rows of bookshelves.

"Al," Henrietta called after him, "is time ever weird down here?"

"Time?" said Al, rummaging through the stacks.

"Does it seem not to pass down here?"

"Sometimes," Al's voice came, "I'm down here for what seems like hours with these old books, and I'll get hungry for dinner, and head upstairs, and find that your grandmother—"

His voice cut off suddenly. Henrietta ran back to see what was the matter. She found him stooped over, having just removed a book from a low shelf. He was holding one hand to his forehead, and his eyes were squeezed shut. Henrietta's heart skipped a beat. Al turned and Henrietta saw tears on his cheeks. "I'm sorry, Henrietta. I'm grieving."

"Grieving?" said Henrietta.

Al paused. "Did your parents not tell you?" he asked, his brow furrowing. "Your grandmother—my Henrie—passed away."

"Oh," said Henrietta. She felt a lump in her throat.

"Henrietta . . ." Gary's voice from the main room sounded urgent. "Henrietta!" he shrieked. Then, there was a soft thud.

Henrietta and Al both raced out to see that the Wikkeling had somehow managed to reach the bottom of the staircase. Its arm had snapped out again, and its finger was now locked to Gary's forehead. Gary lay unconscious on the floor, his face pale.

Distress Call

Henrietta didn't know she was rushing at the Wikkeling until Al restrained her. "Let him go!" she screamed at it.

"Henrietta, stop," said Al.

"It's going to kill Gary," she said.

"Look," said Al. He opened the book he'd just retrieved from the stacks. *How To: A Book of Instructions*.

Al paged through the table of contents (*How to Fix a Leaky Faucet; How to Carve a Turkey; How to Stop Time*) and then flipped forward to the chapter he was looking for: How to Attract a Wild Housecat.

They skimmed the entry.

Wild housecats are fascinating, intelligent creatures, but tend to be wary of people. The easiest way to attract a wild housecat is to construct a cat hall—a wild-housecat-sized doorway built into an exterior wall. Some report advantages from framing the hall, writing a welcome message over the lintel, or otherwise giving the hall an inviting appearance. Once the hall is built, wait six to six hundred weeks, during which time it is likely that a wild housecat will appear.

"Six to six *hundred*?" Henrietta exclaimed.

"Keep reading," said Al.

If you are in _immediate_ need, there is an additional method available, although a cat hall must still be installed. Procure a small amount of dried wild housecat blood (obtainable from many Friends of Wild Housecats societies). Dampen the blood with water and apply it to the entrance of the cat hall. When the wind carries the smell of the blood outside, any wild housecat in the vicinity should smell it and come quickly, assuming one of its kind is in danger. Since this method involves attracting these very intelligent and easily perturbed animals through false pretense, you'd best be ready with a good explanation for your actions when the cat arrives.

"We can make a hall," Al said, "but what about the blood?"

Henrietta thought of the blood on the attic floor, in her house . . . and her eyes lit up. "Al!" she said. "Do you still have the textbook I gave you?"

Al loped back into the shelves and emerged with the book in his hands. Henrietta opened it.

There it was: the drop of blood, dry and brown now, that had fallen onto her math problem the night she'd found Mister Lady.

"Amazing!" said Al. There was no time to enjoy their good fortune. Al hurried off into the rear room he'd shown Henrietta on her first visit, where he kept his old tools.

Henrietta looked over at Gary. His lips were closed tight, his face screwed up in pain. The Wikkeling's finger was still attached to his forehead, its long arm snaking back to its body at the base of the stairs.

"We've got to hurry," said Henrietta as Al returned.

"Won't be attractive, but it'll do," said Al. He handed Henrietta a hammer with a large metal head, then plugged a small power saw into a nearby wall socket. "I'll saw through the wall, and you hit it with the hammer to knock it out."

The saw whined loudly as Al revved it, dust flying off the long-unused blade. He pressed it into the wall, at ground level outside, and an awful-looking plume of black smoke poured from the slice. He steered the saw through a neat square cut, and then backed away. "Whack it!" Henrietta struck the square with the hammer and knocked it out onto Al's front yard. Evening air flooded in.

"We've got to dampen the blood," said Al, "and there's no running water down here!"

Henrietta grabbed the textbook, spat on the page, mixed the spit and blood with her finger, and quickly daubed it around the edges of the cat hall.

She and Al turned around just in time to see the Wikkeling's arm retract into its body with a snap, like a measuring tape. It flickered out for a moment, reappeared lying on the ground, blinked out again, and then returned, standing. The proximity to the books seemed to be taking a toll on it.

Henrietta ran to Gary. He was unconscious, but now that the connection to the Wikkeling was broken, he seemed to relax a little bit.

The Wikkeling visibly gathered its strength. It straightened and solidified. The vague circle of its gaping mouth stretched into an empty smile.

The Stink

I f anyone had happened to go strolling past Al's house that night, they would have observed a small chunk of the house's outer wall falling into the lawn in a cloud of black smoke; then, a child's hand appearing and smearing something around the edges.

That mixture of blood and spit began to stink, though too subtly for a human nose to detect. The stink wafted across the plastic green grass to the street. It ascended above rooftops and gusted along highways.

It drifted past OK and Oak, deep in the Old City. After leaving Rose, Henrietta, and Gary in the dumpster, OK had called Rose's parents and told them everything, including the children's destination. Rose's parents called Henrietta's parents and asked them if they knew anyone at Sunset Estates. They did. They called Al, but Al didn't answer. They called Gary's mother.

In this manner it came to pass that Rose's parents Sid and Sigrid, Henrietta's parents Aline and Tom, and Ms. Span all headed toward Al's town house in Sunset Estates, along with several police officers and a fire truck that had been summoned when some black smoke had drifted through Al's neighbor's window.

The stink traveled onward on the wind, past the place you've reached in this story and into the next, and the one after, until it finally encountered a nose sensitive enough to smell it.

Two Wild Housecats

The Wikkeling's smile was the most frightening thing Henrietta had ever seen. Its flickering pink mouth and yellow eyes widened as it raised its arm and pointed its long index finger at her. Its arm began to extend.

"Don't!" Al shouted.

Henrietta scrambled behind the couch. She braced herself.

Then a shadow fell across the cat hall.

A familiar gray head appeared, followed by a pair of shoulders and long legs. Mister Lady leapt silently to the carpeted floor. Then another cat entered. A fat, orange-striped tabby, considerably larger than Mister Lady, squeezed its bulk through, looking strangely dignified as it tumbled down with a graceless *thud*.

The directions in *How To* had said you'd better be ready to explain yourself when the wild housecats show up, but Mister Lady and her ample friend seemed to know exactly why they'd been summoned. Mister Lady crouched and then sprang in a fantastic leap, landing right on the Wikkeling's shoulder. The Wikkeling jerked back, but she clung tenaciously and raised a paw, exposing a set of long, razor-sharp claws. She slashed its face, and the Wikkeling's smile wilted as four pale gashes appeared across its cheek and nose. It winked out of existence for a moment, and Mister Lady fell through to the stairs even as it reappeared a

few steps above her. The orange tabby stood above it near the top landing, arching his back and hissing. Mister Lady, from below, yowled low in her throat, exposing her long, white teeth.

Henrietta had always heard that cats were dangerous, but when she befriended Mister Lady she'd somewhat forgotten those warnings. Now she saw that they could be dangerous indeed when the situation called for it.

The Wikkeling cast about, trapped between the cats. Its face was bleeding profusely, a clear liquid like corn syrup. With one long finger, it stabbed out at the cats as they closed in.

"Look at its legs," said Al. At first, Henrietta wasn't sure what he meant, but then she saw that the Wikkeling's legs had stopped flickering. The yellow fabric of its pants was cracking at the folds, like clay.

The Wikkeling began to sweat as it turned upstairs and down, desperately seeking escape, and its face shone in the fluorescent lights. Soon its clothing was wet as well, as if slicked in mud.

"It's getting younger," said Henrietta. Except for its long hands and fingers, which dangled enormously, the Wikkeling was no longer full-grown. Even as she watched, its stature shrank until it appeared as she'd seen it through the attic windows: a monstrous child.

Next to Henrietta, Rose stirred and sat up. Henrietta held her hand, and together they watched the awful reduction of their tormentor. The child Wikkeling's mouth opened and closed, but no sound emerged, just the flickering light in the back of its throat. It looked terrified, desperate.

"What's it saying?" said Henrietta.

"I can't hear," said Al.

Whatever it was, the Wikkeling repeated it over and over. As it continued to shrink, its features dislodged from their positions on its face. Its mouth drifted up onto its cheek, and its teeth dribbled down its neck. The rest of its body lost cohesion and spread out over the stairs, mixing with its clothes into a yellow soup. In mere moments, only a lumpy puddle remained, with a pair of eyes sinking into it. Then, nothing.

The wild housecats stepped toward one another and sat together on the now empty stair. Mister Lady licked the ear of the tabby and straightened his fur fussily with one paw.

Rose went to Gary. His hands, which had been balled in tight fists, loosened. His eyes opened. "What happened?" he gasped, sitting up quickly.

"The Wikkeling evaporated," said Rose.

Henrietta turned toward the cats to thank them, but saw only the flick of a gray tail at the edge of the cat door as Mister Lady disappeared after her friend. It was as if they'd stopped by on their way to another engagement—which may indeed have been the case.

Then a knock sounded from upstairs, and a cheerful rendition of "Jingle Bells" began.

"Someone's here," said Al.

Lots of someones, in fact: Henrietta's parents, Rose's parents, Gary's mother, ten police officers, two police dogs, and five firefighters were crowded on the porch, waiting for some explanations.

Explanations

The children realized that an honest account of their experiences wouldn't be well-received, so they chimed in on an improvised medley of conflicting fabrications (each confirmed by a bemused but willing Al), and the following story emerged:

Henrietta, Gary, and Rose had wanted to borrow some books from Al. Because Henrietta was grounded, they decided to sneak out her bedroom window. They caught a public bus, but accidentally boarded the wrong one and also accidently dropped their phones while trying to call for help. Humiliated and phoneless, they'd ended up at Sunset Estates just as Al was sawing through his wall to . . . deal with . . . an electrical problem.

Of the crowd assembled at Al's door, the firefighters were the first to leave, since there was no fire. The police officers departed next, since there was no crime.

Rose's parents followed, with Rose in tow. They were upset at her, but they knew there was more to the story and that Rose would tell them the details once they'd returned to the Library.

Ms. Span and Gary made their exit. Gary would be grounded for a week. Unlike Rose, he would not be explaining the real story to his mother. To her, the truth would sound more like a lie than the lies did. There was one thing Gary did want to come clean about, however. As he sat next to his mother while she drove them home, he clenched his hands, collecting his courage. "Mom, I have to tell you something."

"Are you going to explain why you smell like a garbage pile?" his mother said, turning to eye his pockets as she spoke. "You haven't been collecting again, have you? You know I've expressly forbidden it."

"Oh," Gary said, putting his hands around his waist. "I think I sat in something." In fact, his pockets were bulging with some amazing pieces he'd discovered during the garbage truck ride, which he could hardly wait to catalog.

"You'll scrub the seat when you get home, and shower after that," said her mother briskly.

"Mom, what I wanted to say is . . ." Gary cleared his throat. "I had a secret. I've been keeping it a long time, but it isn't a secret anymore. So I want to tell you."

"Oh," said Ms. Span, and her face showed some concern.

"I can't . . . I mean, I *couldn't* . . . read."

"What?" she said. "Don't joke, Gary. Of course you can read."

"I can now," said Gary, "but not until this year. I used to cheat. But I'm learning—Henrietta and Rose have been helping me."

"*Henrietta* has been helping *you?*" said Ms. Span, aghast.

Gary insisted on his story, and somehow—through exhaustion, relief, or too much worry in one day—his mother finally believed him. "Beginning tomorrow, you and I are going to have supervised study sessions after dinner," she said crisply.

"Okay," said Gary happily, flicking a bit of eggshell from the leg of his pants and onto the pristine car floor.

●·· ··●

After Gary and his mother left, a long, awkward silence ensued between Henrietta, her parents, and Al.

"Mom," said Henrietta. "I'm sorry."

"Sweetie," her mother sighed. She looked worn-out and sad. "That was a terrible, dangerous thing to do. I have no idea what you were thinking. But I'm glad you're all right."

"You're still grounded, though," said her father. Then he almost smiled. He gathered Henrietta in for a hug, but just as quickly released her, waving a hand in front of his face. "You smell awful," he said.

Henrietta's mother sniffed the air. "That's coming from you?"

Henrietta shrugged.

Then Al spoke up, looking uncomfortable. "Aline," he said, "we need to talk."

Henrietta's mother tensed up. She folded her arms across her chest and looked impatient. "I'm not sure what you mean," she said.

Al's face clouded with doubt. "Aline," he said slowly, "you and your parents meant the world to me. They were all I lived for." He paused, took a deep breath and let it out and then continued. "But that world . . . well, it's passing away. I hope it isn't too late. I want things to change. I want . . ." He struggled for words for a moment. "I want to be your father, Aline. For as long as I have left. If you'll have me."

Another long silence fell on the room.

Aline looked at her husband, and then at Henrietta. She closed her eyes, and her face relaxed. Then she stood, crossed the room to Al, and hugged him. As her arms closed around his old shoulders, a grieving sob suddenly escaped her. Al's eyes reddened, and his old, wrinkled face grimaced, which is the only expression you can make when you're feeling too many emotions at once.

The Memorial

The memorial service for Grandmother Henrie was held at the Sunset Estates community center. Henrietta dressed in her nicest pants and wore her uncomfortable dress shoes.

Al and Henrie's elderly friends were there, and they were all terribly nice, and terribly sad—they were often attending funerals these days. During the service, Al stood next to Henrietta and her parents, and it felt strange and new to all of them to be a family.

After the service, everyone gathered at Al's house. For the first time in Henrietta's memory, she and her parents stayed until the very end. They didn't look for an excuse to leave early, and they didn't stand awkwardly and act like they wanted to be elsewhere. Henrietta's father was unexpectedly charming, and her mother was a whiz at learning people's names.

Near the end of the evening, when the remaining guests were chatting in the living room, Henrietta approached Al in the kitchen.

"Grandpa?" she said. Al turned from the counter and smiled as he saw her.

"It's nice to hear you call me that," he said.

"I was wondering if you'd start a book club with me. We aren't using books at school anymore, but I thought we could read some, with my friends. When we aren't grounded anymore."

"I'd like that very much," said Al.

●●·●●

Henrietta and her parents were the last guests to depart, and they helped Al clean up. As they said their good-byes on the front porch, Aline and Al hugged silently. Henrietta heard a sound coming from up the street and turned just in time to see the garbage truck pull through the parking lot. She smiled, even though the sight also made her a little nauseous.

On the drive home, they reflected on the responsibilities that awaited them the next morning. Henrietta would return to school, and her father and mother both had work to do. Of course, life wouldn't be quite so regular as it once was. "Henrietta," said her mother, "there's something I should have mentioned."

Henrietta was thinking about how wonderful it would be to take off her horrid, too tight shoes when she got home. Her feet throbbed. "What is it?" she asked.

"We found out last week that the city wants us to move. Our house is going to be demolished. It's good news, actually. We can go anywhere. I know you've never liked that old place. It made you sick."

"It didn't make me sick, actually," said Henrietta, but she stopped herself quickly from explaining further—the story would be far too strange for her parents to accept.

Her mother continued: "We'll move someplace new. A fancy house like Ms. Span's."

"I want to stay in our house," said Henrietta, firmly. "Can we tell them we don't want to leave?"

"I'm afraid their minds are made up, Henrietta," said her father.

"Could we find another old house, then?" said Henrietta.

Her mother looked over at her father, and they shared a puzzled glance. Their daughter was quite an inexplicable creature. Just then, Henrietta's father's cell phone rang, and he hooked it to his ear by a little ear clip.

"Tom here," he said. "Yes, I—what? I'm sorry, say that again. Elton, am I hearing you right?" Tom frowned. "Elton, I'm going to have to call you back. I'm spending some time with my family right now." He disconnected and returned the phone to his pocket.

"What is it, Tom?" said Aline.

"Just work," said Tom.

"But what?" said Henrietta.

"Tough to explain," he said. This was what he always said, and Henrietta pushed a little further.

"*Try*," she said insistently.

"Well, there's a program called the System Manager. It connects other programs together, you could say. It makes them run efficiently. Anyway, it crashed yesterday, and we've been trying to repair it. Now I just heard that apparently it has deleted itself."

"Deleted?" said Aline.

"That's what I've been told. Needless to say, I'll be going in early tomorrow. But I'm not going to worry about it now."

Henrietta leaned back in her seat and looked out the window at the other lanes of traffic and the buildings that walled the street, shining in the strong glow of the streetlights. She thought about Al's *How To* book. If she did have to move, she thought, the first thing she'd do in the new house would be to build a beautiful cat hall with a painted lintel that read ALL CATS WELCOME across the top.

The Attic Books

Gary and Henrietta were grounded for a week. In Henrietta's case, this involved having no friends over, supervised homework sessions after school, and no personal use of her brand new Skipping-Stone Phone.

It wasn't so bad, though. Henrietta's mother was quite supportive of her efforts to improve her schoolwork, and sitting with her after dinner to complete compositions and math problems was kind of fun. Henrietta hadn't known that her mother was a whiz at math, and she even talked about her own accounting work a little bit, using examples from her job to illustrate some of the problems Henrietta had to work.

But Henrietta immensely missed going into the attic with Gary and Rose. Although they spent time together at school, they couldn't really relax there, Henrietta especially, since she was AT RISK.

Henrietta hadn't been back to the attic since the three of them escaped through the cat hall. Now that the BedCam was working again, and her parents were watching her every move, she hadn't had even a second alone—a deplorable situation, since she'd come to depend on the solitude of the attic to give her time to think about things.

When the day finally dawned that signaled the end of Henrietta's punishment, she awakened not to the sound of her alarm, but to the sound of her phone ringing. She reached out groggily and checked the screen, brightening immediately when she saw the name.

"Grandpa!" she said as she answered.

"Hello, Henrietta," said Al. "Remember how you said you wanted to start a book club? How about tonight?"

Henrietta beamed. "I want to! But I have to ask—"

"I asked already," said Al. "In fact, your friend Rose's mother suggested we meet at their house. I've arranged to pick up you and Gary, if you're interested."

"Yes!" Henrietta shouted.

●•• ••●

School was a blur of typing practices and advice about Halloween (a topic that would continue to wax for weeks in anticipation of the dreaded holiday, including cautionary movies about Jack-O'-Lantern disasters, poison candy, and dangerous strangers). Henrietta worried over all of the Practice Tests because the next Competency Exam could spell the end of her scholastic career.

Soon enough though, the day ended, and Henrietta, Gary, and Rose headed home on the bus. Henrietta quizzed Rose about what her house was like, only to find her mysterious, evasive, and more than a little amused. When the bus arrived at Rose's stop, Rose smiled as she disembarked, saying, "See you later!"

Henrietta ate a distracted dinner in front of the TV with her parents, fielding a few questions about school and apologizing for a mistype she'd made on a composition when she had written "affect" instead of "effect." Nonetheless, her parents seemed pleased with her progress.

When the evening news began, a knock sounded at the side door.

Henrietta jumped up from the couch.

"Have a good time," said her mother.

"I will!" said Henrietta. She exited to the kitchen, opened the door, and hugged her grandfather.

They walked to the car and Henrietta opened the rear passenger door to find Gary already inside, waggling his eyebrows delightedly.

The car crawled through traffic toward Rose's house, Al following the lead of the car's computer. As they drove, they heard an ad about a kind of ice that stayed cold even in ovens. Imagine: a broiled milkshake.

"NOW ARRIVING AT YOUR DESTINATION," said the computer. "TURN LEFT, AND PARK IN THE DRIVEWAY. THESE INSTRUCTIONS BROUGHT TO YOU BY EARHELPERS. WITH EARHELPERS—," Al turned off the engine, and they all stepped onto the driveway, Al holding a few books in one hand that he'd brought for the meeting.

Before them stood an enormous mansion. But its size wasn't the most impressive thing about it. Rather, it was the look of the place. It resembled the old houses Henrietta and Gary had seen through the attic windows, but much, much bigger. The roof wasn't one roof, but many small roofs, sloping down multiple planes and along gables. A turret rose from the middle that appeared constructed from a single old tree trunk.

"It's hu-uge," said Gary, extending the word because "huge" wasn't quite huge enough.

A grand staircase led to a pair of immense double doors, where Al knocked with his free hand. A latch clicked on the other side, and the heavy wood creaked on old hinges. They all took a step back, a little nervous about the imposing place, but their nerves quieted when Rose peeked out, smiling.

"Come in!" she said.

They entered a gigantic sitting room that contained two warmly burning fireplaces, a variety of upholstered chairs scattered in groups, reading desks, and even a study carrel along one wall. At the center of the room stood a long table covered with old maps. Every wall in the place was clothed in bookshelves, which reached to the ceiling far overhead. As the three looked around, awestruck, Rose's parents approached to greet them.

"I'm Sigrid," said Rose's mother. "And I'm Sid," said Rose's father. "It's nice to meet you all officially. Things were a bit rushed the other night."

"It's nice to meet you both," said Al.

"Me, too," said Gary.

"When Rose told us you were starting a book club," said Sigrid, "it seemed sensible to have it here, since we call this house the Library. And as you can see, that's what it is."

"But it didn't used to be," said Al.

"Hm?" said Sid.

"This . . . was . . . ." Al trailed off. He seemed lost in a memory, and he turned in a slow circle, taking everything in. Then he strode to a far corner of the room where two bookcases connected. He knelt and began pulling books from the bottom shelf and peering into the shadows. He laughed. "I can't believe it!" he said.

Everyone joined him, kneeling and looking at the little shadowed spot he

indicated. There, clumsily carved into the wood of the shelf, were three words.
ALBERT WUS HERE

"Albert?" said Henrietta.

"That's me," said Al. "A long, long time ago. Back when this place wasn't a library. It was a *school*. So long ago I'd nearly forgotten, if you can believe that."

"You are pretty old," said Henrietta.

"But it's strange. The school wasn't here in the city. We took a boat to it."

"When we found this house, it was abandoned," said Sid. "You're the first person I've met who knows anything about it."

"I remember sitting here, and talking with a teacher there. I was scolded once over there."

"We should start the meeting," said Rose. "The other members are waiting."

"Other members?" said Gary.

Instead of answering, Rose turned to a wide staircase that ascended from the first level of the house to the second in a broad rightward sweep.

"Have a good time," said Sigrid, as she and Sid disappeared off in another direction.

"My parents will talk to you about this when you leave," said Rose, "but don't tell anyone you were here. And from now on, you'll use the back door. There's a secret knock."

Al's eyebrows raised, but he said nothing. Lately, anything seemed possible. The world was swiftly becoming quite interesting, he reflected. He wished Henrie was alive to see it.

They climbed another staircase once they reached the second floor, walked along a hallway lined with hardback history books to a third staircase, ascended that, turned left, walked through a reading room where several people read books and drank tea from antique cups, and finally arrived in a small corner that contained a nondescript, narrow door.

"I decided to have the meetings up here," said Rose.

"Is this the part that sticks up, outside?" said Gary.

"The turret," said Rose. "I call it the attic. I thought we could call our book club The Attic Books."

She opened the door, revealing an exceedingly narrow, ascending spiral staircase. It was made all of stone.

"This is weird," said Gary, touching his hand to the stone wall. "It looks like wood, but it's rock." The stone was composed of many distinct minerals pressed together in layers that resembled wood grain, some translucent and others opaque.

"It's petrified," said Rose, mounting the steep case. The spiral wound twice and they emerged in a small, circular room lined with books and lit by candles. The walls were made of petrified wood, and it was apparent that the room was the interior of an ancient tree. They'd walked right up the inside of the trunk.

High up on the walls several small windows let in the early evening light. In the middle of the room, a group of six chairs were arranged in a circle. Two were occupied, and their inhabitants stood as the group entered.

"Oak!" said Gary.

"OK!" said Henrietta. And then, "This is my grandfather, Al. Al, this is Oak and OK. They're friends who helped us, even though they look scary."

"Do I look scary?" said OK from behind his gray-streaked beard, his bald head and grocery bag suspenders glinting in the candlelight. Oak couldn't even stand fully upright in the space, he was so massive. His shoulders bulked against the lowest rafters.

"It's nice to meet you both," said Al. He shifted the books he was carrying from his right hand to his left, so he could shake their hands.

"What's that?" said Gary, pointing up at one of the walls. In the space between the tops of the bookshelves and the bottom of the high windows a small wooden sign was set into the stone, which read,

IYCHMN EON

"I don't know," said Rose. "This place is really old."

"Well," said Al, "it's very nice to have everyone together, finally ungrounded! I brought a few books to show you all, if you'd like to start the meeting." Everyone found seats in the circle, and Al put the three books he'd brought on his lap. He held up the first one. "This is Henrietta's textbook from school," he said. He flipped through the plastic pages. "I'd call this a modern book. It's unusual because it has a spot of wild housecat blood between two pages. It was probably only printed a year or so ago, but it already has an interesting history." He handed Henrietta's textbook to Oak. "The second book I brought is very old. It's one of Aristotle Alcott's journals." Al showed the old, softcover book. Its pages were crumbling, the leather spine cracked. OK immediately held out his hands for it, and Al gave it to him.

"This is the same Alcott who made the *Bestiary*?" OK asked, opening the journal carefully and looking into the handwritten interior.

"The same," said Al. "It's the oldest book I own. I would call it ancient."

OK passed the book to Rose, who turned it gently over in her hands.

"This could use conservation," she said. Al gave her a questioning look. "Repair."

"Rose can fix any book that ever was," said Gary. "She's an expert."

"I didn't know books could be fixed," said Al.

"I didn't either," said Henrietta, "but Rose even repaired the *Bestiary*."

"I'll do it this week," said Rose.

"The final book I brought today," said Al, "was one I'd almost completely forgotten about. It's neither modern nor ancient. I'll call it 'old' because I think it's about my age. I'd like to nominate it as our first book club assignment."

Al showed everyone this final, slim volume, which immediately reminded Henrietta of *Early Town*. She read the title in the shifting candlelight:

THE WIKKELING:
Fact or Fairy Tale?

"Where did you *get* that?" said Gary, aghast.

"I don't remember," said Al. "I've owned it for many years. In fact, I have two copies, so we can share it."

"Maybe we have one at the Library, too," said Rose. "I'll ask my mom and dad."

"There are three different times," Henrietta mused. "The present, the past, and the ancient past."

"So I'm in the present," Gary said, "and the past is through the windows, and I think about the *ancient* past when I see the big stump."

Al looked at him curiously. "What are you referring to?"

"Well . . . ." said Henrietta. And, as it seemed as good a time as any, she told the story. Gary and Rose both chimed in too, adding details here and there and occasionally contradicting one another a little bit—but not much. The facts were plain. As the tale unwound, Al, Oak, and OK listened raptly.

"Things are coming together," said Al. "You say that the Wikkeling started making you sick when it couldn't find you. In this book," Al indicated *Wikkeling: Fact or Fairy Tale*, "it says that the Wikkeling was originally created to destroy a dangerous animal, called the Draageling. To bring the Wikkeling to life, the scientists placed a slip of paper in its mouth with a secret word written on it. Do you know what the word was?" Al paused dramatically, and when no one conjectured he said, "It was *grow*."

"I don't understand," said Gary.

"I wonder if that's what it was repeating as it melted," said Rose.

"I think I see now," said Henrietta. "When it taps people, it's feeding from them somehow, and it's always hungry because it's growing."

"And it couldn't reach us in our old houses, or in the attic," said Gary. "So it got mad?"

"Maybe it didn't even mean to make us sick," said Henrietta. "It was just upset—like how our parents grounded us when they found us at Al's. Even the Competency Exam makes sense! All the subtraction problems turned into addition."

"It would hate subtraction, if it only wants to grow," said Gary.

"And it would love addition," said Henrietta.

Then Rose, who had been silent for some time, spoke up. "This whole city is called the Addition," she said. This statement stopped the conversation in its tracks for a few moments.

"Well, we've certainly got plenty to think about," said Al. "But we also have the tools to do it. Oh, and here's something else." He opened the book and showed everyone the inside of the front cover. At the top of the page was written,

THIS BOOK HAS BEEN READ BY:

The rest of the page was ruled with lines, like notebook paper. The first seven or so had names written on them, some in pen, some in pencil, some cursive, some printed. The remainder were blank. "I have several books like this," said Al. "People used to write their names in when they finished reading, and you could see who'd had it before you. Since I read this one last week, I added my name at the bottom." He handed the book to Henrietta. "You'll write yours next," he said.

Back to the Attic

After the meeting, Al drove Henrietta home, and she entered the living room to find her mother watching television alone. The late news was on, and Henrietta sat next to her.

In the top story, a man had been eaten by a bear, deep in the Old City. The only thing the bear didn't swallow, the solemn shellac-haired newscaster told the camera, was the man's mouth. "The police report that the mouth was still screaming when they found it," he said. An ad came on after, and Henrietta's mother muted it.

"Henrietta," she said, "if you ever see a bear, call an adult."

"I will," said Henrietta.

"How was your book club?"

"It was fun," said Henrietta. "We decided on a book to read."

"Does it contain District-Approved Vocabulary?" said her mother.

"Yes," said Henrietta.

The news returned for a final story about research being done on a new cell phone that would be implanted directly into the subscriber's brain. "We'll all have instant access to everyone, all the time," the newscaster chirped gleefully, twirling his finger at his own head.

"We just bought that spot today," said Henrietta's father, emerging from the hallway.

"What's the phone going to be called?" said Henrietta's mother.

"We're leaning toward *Perpetuality*."

"That's got a nice ring to it."

"Pun intended?"

Henrietta saw beads of sweat on her father's forehead, as if he'd been working on something.

"What are you doing, dad?" she asked.

"Your BedCam is broken again," said her father. "I swear, I'm looking forward to this old place getting torn down!"

Henrietta's eyes widened. "I have homework to do!" she blurted, and she ran down the hallway, her mother calling after her, "It's almost bedtime!"

Henrietta closed her bedroom door and lifted her chair onto her desk. She climbed up past the broken eye of the BedCam, pressed her hands against the seam, and at long last entered the attic.

●·· ··●

It was perfectly quiet and dark now that the windows were sealed off. Henrietta lit the candles in the candelabra and closed the trapdoor. She wondered if the moon was shining right now on that other town, lighting the bricks of its old street, or if those bricks had already been paved over.

Her eyes fell on the brown stain next to the trapdoor. It seemed like forever ago when she'd found this place. It seemed, furthermore, like a story about someone else. And she *was* a different person then. Everything that had happened since had changed that girl into the person she was now.

A small noise came from behind her, interrupting her thoughts. She turned and searched the deep shadows cast by the candles. Her eyes traveled up the tallest bookcase. A familiar form was illuminated there by the candlelight.

Mister Lady jumped down and alighted easily on the armrest on the far end of the couch. She looked at Henrietta with her enormous eyes—clear green, like new leaves.

Henrietta's heart leapt. She wanted to spring from her seat and throw her arms around the cat. She wanted to rub her ears and kiss her between the eyes, and hold her soft paws in her hands. But instead she sat quietly.

If you or I had seen her, we might have thought Henrietta was afraid.

She wasn't, though. She was simply a considerate person—one who knew that wild animals don't like to be petted, even if you and they are friends.